Tara's Sister Trouble

Quercus

First published in Great Britain in 2014 by

Quercus Editions Ltd
55 Baker Street
7th Floor, South Block
London
W1U 8EW

A CIP catalogue reference for this book is available
from the British Library

Paperback ISBN: 978 1 78206 980 5
Ebook ISBN: 978 1 78206 981 2

10 9 8 7 6 5 4 3 2 1

Typeset in Perpetua by IDSUK (DataConnection) Ltd
Printed and bound in Great Britain by Clays Ltd, St Ives plc.

For my husband.
'It's just so easy.'

Prologue

'The first rule of Gorgeous Guy Safari,' I say, making binoculars with my fingers and holding them up to my eyes, 'is complete silence until you spot a target.'

Abby and Maxie giggle. Like most weekends, I'm hanging out with my best friend and my sister. We're on the first floor of the shopping centre, looking down to the floor below.

'That particular species is extinct at my school,' says Maxie.

'That's a bit lame,' says Abby. 'Hasn't even one of them revealed their secret hotness under their geeky exterior?'

'Ooh, Clark Kent-style,' I say. 'Genius by day, hunky by night.'

Everyone at Maxie's school is a genius, even Maxie. She's a bona fide, one-hundred-per-cent gifted, born-with-it genius, who can multiply *x*s and *y*s to somehow make real numbers. She goes to a special school for gifted children. It's kind of cool that my sister's a mastermind, but the bad part is that her school is much nearer Dad's. She lives at his house during the week and we only get to see each other weekends – one at Dad's and one at Mum's. We're still really close though. We have been all our lives. Even more so since the divorce.

'Maybe one or two of the boys are nice. I haven't really noticed.' Maxie's not really into boys yet.

Her face falls into a grungy scowl. 'School is a bit lame too . . .' Her voice lowers and she closes her eyes for a little too long. 'I've been moved down a set in English. Again.'

Not again! I feel a terrible whack of guilt. This might be my fault.

'Get Tara to help,' Abby says, tapping my arm. 'You'll help your big sister, won't you?'

Quick, change the subject. 'She's not really my *big sister*,' I say. Maxie is only eleven months older than me. Probably why we've always got on despite the fact we're so different. I think Maxie would look fab in my pink Roxy top, but she's wearing her favourite gigantic black jumper with holes in it, over skinny jeans a size too big. They keep falling down. Although I hate the overgrown jumper, I love my sister. I miss her so much when she's at Dad's. I miss them both.

Suddenly, a member of the male species catches my eye, one with floppy brown hair. I zoom my binoculars round to get a better look.

It's him!

My stomach instantly goes heavy, as if my throat has fallen into it. There's a specific bounce to his walk. I can even identify him from ten metres up, just from looking at the back of his head.

'Hey. Isn't that Reece over there?' says Abby, putting up her finger binoculars as well.

'The boy from Rimewood School who lives near Mum's?' asks Maxie, stepping back from the rail so he doesn't catch her looking. 'Didn't you have a crush on him?'

Abby nods. 'He used to walk Tara home every day.'

'Only because it was on his way,' I say. I didn't know if he walked me home because he liked me or because he *liked* me. Now I'll never know. He moved to Hillcrest High in at the start of Year 7.

'Poor, heartbroken Tara,' says Abby.

'I wouldn't exactly say *heartbroken*,' I reply. 'I wouldn't exactly call drawing hearts with large cracks in them and the letters *RL* in the middle *heartbroken*.'

Abby and Maxie giggle at my broken heart. I'm joking, but actually I still think about Reece all the time.

Abby whispers, 'Shall we shout something?'

'No,' says Maxie, pulling at a strand of her greasy hair. She hates speaking to strangers.

'Nooooo,' I say. But really I'd love to. It's been ages since I bumped into him.

None of us is brave enough to do anything, but suddenly Reece looks up – clearly sensing the crosshairs on the back of his head. I duck behind the balcony, but it's made of glass so he sees me ducking.

He waves. I drop my binoculars.

He runs towards the escalator and we straighten up.

'How do I look?' I ask the girls.

Abby gives me a thumbs-up.

'You look good,' says Maxie, her grungy scowl reaching a new level of nervousness.

'Hi, Tara,' Reece says, as he walks over from the escalator. He's wearing a hoody and really baggy trousers. 'Hi, Abby. How are you?'

Maxie has gone red, not looking up from her feet. I give her a helping hand. 'Do you know my sister, Maxine?' I ask him.

He frowns. 'Did you go to Rimewood?' he asks.

'I . . . er . . . for . . . yes. For a bit,' she says.

Good one, Max.

'You were in the year above us, weren't you?'

Even though she should have been in our year, Maxie was put in a year ahead.

Abby speaks up. 'Maxie goes to—'

Maxie gives her a wide-eyed look, pleading with her not to say.

'Maxie goes to a different school,' I finish for her.

I don't know why Maxie hates people knowing she's special. I would love to be special like her.

'Talking of schools . . .' says Reece. 'Guess what my parents got through the post today from Hillcrest.'

I shrug. There's nothing uglier than a shrug. I want to kick myself.

'Apparently, next year Hillcrest is taking on girls,' he says.

What?!!!

'Pardon me?' I say, pushing down the volcano of excitement threatening to erupt.

Abby takes my hand and squeezes it. She knows how huge this is.

'Yeah,' he says. 'For whatever reason, Hillcrest doesn't want to be just a boys' school any more. I guess they want more pupils, or better results, or whatever. Anyway, they're allowing girls to enrol. Next year, in our year – Year 8. Cool, eh?'

A school filled with boys; a school filled with Reece. It's what heaven must be like. This could be my chance to go to a special school. Not special like my sister's, but definitely special.

'Very cool,' I say, trying not to lose it.

Abby looks at me. 'Do you think your mum would let you join?'

'I don't know,' I say slowly. I feel a pang of doubt. Do I want to go to a school where I'd be surrounded by boys? Do I want to leave everything I know at Rimewood? I'd have to take the exams to get in. I'd have to work hard.

'No harm in asking,' Maxie says. She whispers in my ear. '*I think he really wants you to.*'

'I'll ask too,' says Abby. 'I don't want to stay at Rimewood if you're not there.'

It's a big decision. Should I do this?

'You should totally do it, Tara,' says Reece.

And that's me decided. Tonight I'm going to ask my parents if I can join a boys' school.

Chapter 1

8 months later . . .

'OK, girls, say *cheese*!'

We huddle together in the corridor. Me and these girls I hardly know. I met most of them for the first time about half an hour ago and I'm trying desperately to remember all their names. There's Curly Blonde Candy, with the freckles and about seventeen home-made scoobie bracelets up her arm, and the girl with the long, long hair and hippy beads under the neck of her school uniform. I can't remember her name. It's a weird one, some place in America.

The flash goes off. 'Very nice,' says Mrs Martin.

'Will you take one with mine please, miss?' I ask, and most of the girls rush forward and give her their phones too. We all want a photo for ourselves.

Back in the huddle, Abby puts her arm around me. 'Can you believe that on Monday this will be our actual school?' she says. 'Are you ready?'

'Is a bikini ready for summer?!' I say, trying not to let my nerves show.

Almost a thousand boys go to this school. A thousand of them, and only . . . I turn around to count the girls who are squeezed in around me . . . only nine of us.

'Are *you* ready?' I ask her back.

But I am the luckiest of the girls because I have Abby.

'Is a prisoner ready for the firing squad?' Abby groans.

Oh. Perhaps she's just as nervous as I am. I give her arm a little squeeze.

It's scary but also exciting going to a new school that's different from normal. My sister got into *her* school because she's clever. We did have to pass an entrance exam for Hillcrest, but the main reason I got in is because I'm a girl. I'll never be able to do anything as good as Maxie.

It's been nice to have something else to focus on rather than my sister, even if it *is* scary. Maxie has . . . *changed* over the last few months. We used to be such good friends, but lately she's been horrible to me. I would take it personally, but she's mean to everyone now. She's not thirteen for a few weeks yet, but it's like the teenage tantrums have kicked in early. She's become a *nightmare*.

Worst thing is, we're not even close any more.

'Come on then,' Mrs Martin says, snapping me out of my thoughts as she hands all our phones back. 'Time to meet your new classmates.'

We shuffle towards the assembly-hall door in a group. Abby and I exchange terrified looks. This is it – the moment when we meet the boys we'll be spending the rest of our school lives with. I take a deep breath and glance over at Hannah, with the super-high ponytail. And the girl with the American name – that's it: *Indiana*. They both look pretty nervous too. There's one girl – Simone, I think her name is – who doesn't look scared at all. She looks like a ghost, just wafting along. How can she be so relaxed?

Next to her is Donna Woods and the less said about her, the better. 'Stand aside, ladies,' she whispers. 'I'll go first. Give the boys a good impression.'

Donna's the only other one here who also went to school with me and Abby. But we weren't friends. *Her* best friend is her mirror. I always just ignored her. But when Abby and I said we were leaving to join a boys' school, we got a tiny bit of attention from our class. Next thing we knew, Donna had signed up too. With only nine girls in the year, she's going to be a lot harder to ignore.

She flips a thick brunette lock of hair from her face, and as much as I hate her, I have to admit she looks really pretty.

Mrs Martin opens the door to the hall and we walk in from the back. The hundred or so boys from the year are all sitting in there, all facing forward so I can only see their hair. It's like an advert for a boy factory – all wearing the same uniform. Some blond, some dark, but all Year 8.

But I already know my favourite.

I look around for Reece. *Where is he?*

'I have asked the boys to make sure there are some chairs for you,' Mrs Martin tells us.

The hall is arranged in rows of chairs with an aisle down the middle, and there are a few empty seats left. I look for two empty ones together because I'm not ready to sit next to a boy yet. I'd only ever want to sit next to Abby.

'Gentlemen,' says Mrs Martin, now at the front of the hall, 'thank you for coming in in the summer holidays.'

There's a huffy sigh from some of the boys, probably about the fact they had to wear uniform for one random Wednesday morning in August.

'But the board arranged this Introduction Day. As well as getting your timetables and schedules ready for the term, they thought it would be a good idea if you met your new classmates. I want you to treat them no differently than you would each other.'

'I don't know about that,' a girl beside me whispers. She has dark skin, her hair is plaited into thick rows and she has a green elastic on the end of each plait. 'I've got two brothers and I wouldn't want to be treated the way Jumoke treats Bem.' She giggles quietly. 'I couldn't cope with the wedgies!'

I laugh behind my hand. 'What's your name again?' I whisper.

'Obi,' she says.

'Hi,' I say, 'I'm Tara.'

'Can I sit next to you?' she asks.

Abby flicks her head round.

'Sorry, Obi,' I tell her. 'I'm sitting next to Abby. We're BFFs from our old school.'

'Fair enough,' says Obi.

'Sit near us though, yeah?'

We're all standing awkwardly near the door.

'Come along, girls,' Mrs Martin says, beckoning us in like baby lambs.

Donna Woods virtually pushes us over as she struts past us down the aisle to the front of the hall, wiggling her hips. In my old school no one ever wanted to sit at the front, but I suppose it's one way to get attention.

Weirdly, the boys stay facing ahead. Donna flips her hair again and extracts a pen and notebook from her bag, still standing, so everyone can see her for as long as possible. She reckoned she was queen of Rimewood, and it looks like she's after the crown here too.

Another girl scuttles after her – I think her name is Sonia – trying to wiggle her bum in the same way, but she looks as if she's recovering from a hip operation. 'Mind if I sit next to you?' she asks Donna. 'Please.'

Donna looks her up and down, then shrugs. 'Sure.' Sonia with the pretty ginger hair has clearly passed the test.

I roll my eyes at Abby, and she smiles knowingly. I move to the nearest pair of seats. 'Shall we sit here?'

There's a spare chair behind us and Obi moves to take it.

Abby plonks her bum on her chair – then squeals and jumps right up again. 'It's wet!' There's a big damp patch on the back of her skirt like she's peed herself.

Despite Abby's loud squeal, the boys are *still* facing forward. Now it's starting to make sense. One of them laughs but tries to make it sound like a cough.

'Stop!' I shout. 'Don't sit down.' The rest of the girls hover over the empty seats. I pat my chair and it's wet too. I look back at where Obi is about to sit.

Obi puts her hand on the seat and nods. 'Soaked.'

Now the boys start laughing. Hard. One of them, a skinny, spotty boy, even slaps his knee. Who *does* that in real life?

I put my arm around Abby. Her lip starts to wobble. It would be so bad if she cried in front of everyone when it's not even the first day yet. I glare at the boys. I see Donna is laughing as well so I glare at her too. She wouldn't find it so funny if *she* had been the first to sit down instead of faffing with her bag.

'Abby, dear,' says Mrs Martin, 'why don't you go and use the hand dryer on your skirt. It shouldn't take a minute to dry off.'

Abby runs from the hall. I'm so angry for her. Clearly being a girl in an all-boys' school isn't going to make us special. It's going to make us the enemy. Well, if that's how they want it, that's how they're going to get it.

'Look at the fat girl run,' the spotty boy mutters, making the boy with the square haircut next to him laugh harder.

I turn on them. 'Abby is *not* fat!' I hiss. She's curvy, and beautiful. But she's got a complex about her weight, and this boy is not helping.

'Ha!' he laughs. 'Flabby Abby!'

I scowl.

'Craig Hurst!' Mrs Martin snaps at him. 'Go and get some paper towels and clean every one of the wet chairs for the girls.'

‘But, *miss*,’ he moans, ‘it wasn’t me.’

From the way the boy sitting next to him is sniggering, I can tell it absolutely *was* him.

‘*And* you can stay after everyone has gone, to stack the chairs.’

That shuts Craig Hurst up, and the rest of them too.

By the time our chairs are dry, Mrs Martin has handed out books and timetables.

‘This term is going to be very exciting,’ she says, ‘and not only because we have become a mixed school this year. The board has signed Year 8 up to a fundraising programme. You can raise money for any charity you like.’

That does sound like fun! But the looks on the boys’ faces reveal they don’t feel the same way. One of them carries on flicking his ruler as if he hasn’t even heard.

‘And we thought we’d make a competition out of it. The student, or students, who raise the most money will get a pass for ten people to go to Alton Towers—’

Now the boys are excited. All of them start whooping and talking.

Mrs Martin raises her voice. 'All funds need to be handed in by the end of the month, so you haven't got long. But we have so many ingenious girls and boys in the year that I'm sure you'll find very clever ways to raise money.'

I start thinking of a million things I could do: a raffle, an auction, a dog-walking service . . .

'I think we have an unfair advantage, miss,' Craig pipes up.

'Why's that?' Mrs Martin says.

'Everyone knows that boys' brains are bigger than girls'.'

'Craig. Outside the door. Now.' She marches him out of the hall but he doesn't seem that bothered. I want to do anything I can to wipe that stupid smile off his face. *Boys cleverer than girls?* Not. A. Chance.

We're going to have to show them what we can do. We're going to have to stick together to survive.

Girls against boys.

Suddenly I have it! Abby's still not here so I lean back and speak to Obi. 'We should team up.'

She frowns for a second. 'Do you think we'd be allowed?'

'Why not? Mrs Martin said *student or students*. And the prize is for ten people.'

'A fundraising club?' says Obi.

'Yeah,' I say. 'Me, you and Abby. We can raise money *and* have fun hanging out.'

Mrs Martin comes back in so we have to be quiet.

'Let's meet in the loos to make plans,' I whisper quickly.

Obi nods.

Mrs Martin claps to get our attention. 'That's enough excitement for one day,' she says. 'In a minute you'll—'

The door bangs open. The boy who walks in has hair that's a floppy brown mess, his shirt is half out of his trousers and his striped tie is all the way to one side. I feel my stomach go heavy. It happens every time I see him.

Reece.

'Sorry I'm late, Mrs Martin,' he says, finding an empty chair at the back. 'But I forgot we had to come in today.'

'That's fine, Reece.' Mrs Martin sighs. She looks as if she's had enough of her students, and school hasn't even started yet.

Reece scans round the room. 'So . . .' His eyes register all the girls. 'This is new.'

Everyone laughs, and he's somehow managed to break the tension that's been in the air since we arrived.

Then we make eye contact and he waves hello. Everyone looks at me and I can feel myself blushing. I raise my hand to do a little wave back.

Reece is at Hillcrest. Abby is at Hillcrest. We're starting a club and it already has three members.

I thought it might be scary being a girl in a boys' school. What was I worried about? It's going to be awesome!

Chapter 2

'Abs?' I call, pushing the door to the girls' loos. 'Are you in here?'

Someone pulls a chain inside one of the cubicles. Then Abby walks out, sniffing.

'Have you been crying?' Obi asks gently.

Abby forces a smile on to her face. 'No,' she says with a laugh like *don't be silly*. 'I'm fine.' I think she'd admit she was upset if it was just me and her, but she doesn't want to say in front of Obi.

The girls' loos are brand new, never been used, and they're pretty nice really. Freshly painted, with clean mirrors all along one wall, and the room hasn't picked up that toilet smell that every other school loo has. There are twelve cubicles along the wall, which should be enough given that there are only nine girls in at Hillcrest.

'What did I miss?' Abby asks.

Mrs Martin gave me Abby's timetable and I pass it to her, and I tell her about the fundraising competition and our club idea.

'Can I join?' says Abby.

'Of course!' I tell her. 'We've made you a founder member. And I've had the best idea for the charity we should support.'

Abby raises her eyebrows.

'The Rebecca Gardner Appeal.'

Abby smiles, eyes closed. Rebecca is Abby's sister and she has a condition that affects her kidneys. She's had a million operations and she's going to need a million more. The family have set up a charity which does research into the illness and will also help to buy her a wheelchair.

'Aah, Tara, that's really nice of you,' Abby says.

'Of course,' says Obi. I explained all this to her on the way and she was fully on board.

'Come on,' says Abby. 'Let's get out of here.'

'Hang on . . .'

A space next to the sinks has caught my eye. A little enclave. A sort of *nothing* space. It's about the size of a classroom cupboard, and they could easily have fitted another two loo cubicles there, but I guess, for what ever construction reasons, maybe because of the large pipes in the way, they decided not to.

'This is the perfect place to set up our club meeting room,' I say.

Obi and Abby follow my gaze and see what I'm on about.

'If we hang a sheet across the front. Bring in a couple of cushions. Maybe a box to use as a table – we could make this our own!'

'Fundraising HQ,' says Obi.

'It does mean we definitely can't have any boys in our club,' I say, realizing there's no way we could smuggle Reece into the girls' toilets every break time.

'*Pfft!*' says Obi. 'Who wants boys in our club anyway?'

'Yeah!' says Abby.

'Yeah . . .' I join in. And then inspiration hits. 'It's not a club . . .' I say, 'it's a *mob*.' Sometimes I have to admit I am a bit of a genius. Not like my sister, who is an *actual* genius, but a little bit of a creative genius. '*M.O.B.*,' I explain. 'Mates Over Boys.'

'Love it!' says Abby. She gives me a high five, and Obi high-fives us both.

'Mates Over Boys is going to be the best club ever,' says Abby.

The club needs some work though, to figure out logos and manifestos and badges – not to mention how we're going to raise money and win the competition. Suddenly I have an idea, and I whisper it to Abby. She grins and nods.

'Hey, Obi,' I say. 'It's my birthday tomorrow, and Abby is sleeping over at mine. Do you want to stay too? We can start the club officially.'

Obi doesn't hesitate for a second. 'I'm there.'

With me, Abby and Obi, our Mob is going to be indestructible!

Chapter 3

Abby picks up the large piece of paper she's been working on. It's a poster with 'MOB' and 'Mates Over Boys' written in big fat marker pen.

'I've even thought of a logo.' She points to the top right corner where she's drawn a star with 'M.O.B.' written over it in cool writing. 'But if you don't like it . . .'

'It's awesome,' I tell her.

'And we can stick photos of us on the poster,' she says.

'Cool,' says Obi.

We're all sitting cross-legged on sleeping bags on my bedroom floor at our first ever Mob sleep-over. We made a birthday cake but never got round to baking it. Abby thought it would be fun just to eat the batter. I feel full and sick. It wasn't one of Abby's cleverest suggestions.

'We should also make one of those fundraising thermometer things,' I say.

'Good idea,' says Obi. 'We'll *definitely* raise more money than Donna Woods.'

School hasn't even started, but Obi's smart enough to have worked out the deal with Donna Woods. An hour after we left the introduction day, Donna friended us all on Facebook and posted the photo of all us new girls. I only accepted her friend request because Obi said she was boasting about raising the most money in the competition.

'If she wins the trip to Alton Towers, there's no justice in the world,' Obi continues.

'She won't. There is only one of her,' I say. 'We're clubbing together.'

'Literally!' says Obi.

'I reckon we should see who else wants to join our Mob,' I say. 'Make sure we beat those boys.'

Obi smiles wickedly. 'We should put some tough initiation tests in place!'

I nod, pulling a solemn frown. 'They must prove themselves worthy.'

'And I was thinking . . .' says Abby.

'Don't strain yourself,' I interrupt with a giggle.

Abby clears her throat. 'I was thinking about what else this club needs . . .' She leans in. 'A secret code.' She half whispers the words. 'So the boys can't copy our ideas.'

The only code I've ever had was with my sister. We'd make people think we were psychic by cunningly spelling out words in our conversations. It's an easy trick – we've pulled it on Abby loads of times and she's always totally fooled. Maxie and I haven't done it for ages, but I'd still feel disloyal sharing it with these two.

Luckily I don't have to, as Obi's got another one. 'What about a substitution code?' She grabs a piece of paper from my A4 pad and starts writing on it:

'The Secret Mob Code', she puts at the top, and underlines it.

'You write out the alphabet in full,' she says, scribbling letters across the page. 'Then you pick a number, say five. Then underneath you write out the alphabet again, only with the letter *A* starting four places forward so *A* becomes *E*, *B* becomes *F*, *C* becomes *G* . . . and so on.'

'That's brilliant!' Abby says. I totally agree.

Obi gives me a piece of paper. 'Write a secret message,' she says.

I study the code carefully, and write:

IWPAO KRAN XKUO BKNARAN
Mates Over Boys forever

They're both watching me, and I can tell they're working out what I'm saying as I write it, because Obi gives Abby a high five and shouts, 'Hell, yeah!'

The front door shuts all the way downstairs. 'Tara, sweetie, I'm home!' It's Mum. 'Would you come here for a moment, please?'

I beam at my friends. 'I bet she's got us take-away for my birthday,' I say, suddenly not feeling quite so full or so sick.

Abby claps her hands. 'Hope it's pizza!' she says.

My bedroom is at the top of the house in the loft. I leave Abby and Obi and run down the two flights of stairs to the kitchen. Mum has a big smile on her face, but her cheeks are a bit blurry. Has she been crying? 'I have a surprise for you,' she says.

The surprise is hiding behind Mum. It's not a takeaway. It's Maxie.

What's she doing here? It's Thursday today and she's supposed to be at Dad's.

'Surprise,' Maxie says flatly. 'Happy birthday, Tara.'

But nothing about Maxie looks happy right now.

'Hi, twin,' I say, our old tradition. But she still won't smile.

For thirty days of the year my sister and I are the same age. My birthday is 31 August, hers is 30 September. Maxie is exactly eleven months older than me. Today is my birthday, the day we become twins – both of us twelve. The same age, but we've never acted or dressed the same.

Or, at least, we didn't dress the same until just now.

Mum and Maxie are both carrying bulging shopping bags from Primark and Topshop. Mum must have taken Maxie to a salon as well because her hair looks amazing. It's still long, but it's in layers, with blonde highlights at the front and a new fringe. She pushes it behind one shoulder and looks . . . really cool. I've been saying for ages how I want to get a fringe and, seeing it on Maxie, I realize it would really suit me.

'When you said you were going to be out today,' I say to Mum, 'I didn't realize you were meeting Maxie.' I turn to my sister. 'How come you're not at Dad's?'

'Charming,' she says with a huff.

'I didn't mean it like that,' I say in a small voice.

Except I sort of did. Because although I miss Maxie, recently too much of her is not a good thing.

'Tara.' Mum steps between us, like a policeman trying to break up a fight before it starts. 'Maxie's going through a bit of a tough time.'

I peer around Mum at Maxie, who's now leaning against the kitchen counter pulling at the lengths of her new fringe.

'Are you OK, Max?' I ask.

'Fine.'

Doesn't look like it.

Mum puts her arm around me and walks me a few steps away. 'I know you're officially the younger sister, but we're all going to have to be extra, super-nice to Maxie for a while. Can you do that for me?'

'Of course!' I'd do anything for Maxie. I've done more for her than she even knows.

'Thank you,' says Mum.

'What's happened?' I'm worried now. 'Is it Dad?'

'No, no, he's fine,' she says, and her smile makes me feel better for a moment. But then it drops and the moment is gone. 'It's all a bit complicated right now and we're trying to work it out. But I'll explain soon, OK?'

I nod quickly. I hate that Maxie might be hurting in some way. This could explain why she's been acting so weird over the past few months. Mum reckoned it was puberty. This seems like something more.

There's some material sticking out of the bin – is *that* . . . ? It looks like Maxie's gigantic black jumper with the holes in it. Why would she throw it away? It's her favourite.

'Hear that, Maxie?' Mum turns to Maxie, who is glaring at us like we're about to make her wear one of my pink prom dresses. 'Tara's going to let you join her friends for her birthday party.'

Did I say that?

I never used to mind when Maxie hung out with me. But my sister has changed. And I need some bonding time with my new friends. Some things I want just for myself, without my genius older sister coming in and being better at it than me.

'Yeah, Maxie, we're twins today,' I say with a laugh. 'For the next few weeks we're both twelve . . .' But I'm stopped in my tracks as Maxie pulls a sickly sweet expression and makes a snapping mouth out of her hand, taking the mick out of me talking. 'Twins . . . share . . . things . . .' I say for Mum's benefit, but Maxie is still mimicking me, laughing silently.

'How nice,' Mum says to Maxie, and Maxie instantly straightens her face. 'Tara wants you to join her club!'

I *never* said that! I definitely don't want Maxie in my club, not with the way she's acting. Time for some reverse psychology.

'You can join our club if you want to, Maxie,' I say. I look at her, willing her to make the right decision. 'But we are younger than you – you might think it's stupid.'

Behind Mum's back, Maxie narrows her eyes and nods. She clearly thinks it *is* stupid.

'And it's kind of a school thing,' I add.

The way I figure it, one of three things could happen: option 1 – Maxie refuses to join; option 2 – she joins, goes back to her old self and is really, really nice to be with; option 3 – she acts like the complete Maxie nightmare she's become.

'Thanks, Tara, you're the best! I'd love to join your super-cool club!' she says in a squeaky, TV-presenter voice.

'Isn't that wonderful?' says Mum. But she's faking it too. Something's going on and I can tell she's trying to make everything OK when it's clearly, plainly, not.

I don't know what's going on with Maxie, but my guess is she's going to go for option 3. My birthday sleepover is going to be a nightmare.

Chapter 4

Maxie's in my bedroom, checking out the club poster as she sticks her finger in the bowl of cake mix.

'I thought you said your sister was weird,' whispers Obi.

I said she was immature. But today Maxie's got a little bit of make-up on – mascara, lip gloss and blusher – this is a first.

'She's not weird,' Obi whispers again. 'She looks just like you.'

Maxie spins round, making Obi jump. 'So what do you guys do in your *awesome club*?' she says in an exaggerated American accent.

Maxie doesn't deserve to be in Mates Over Boys. These days I don't think she would put her mates over anything. I'm not sure she even has any mates at Wokingham School for the Gifted. She never brings anyone over.

'Club stuff,' I tell her.

'Well, duh,' she says.

The hoody she's wearing is exactly the same one that I've got, short at the waist with big pockets and a logo on the back – only hers is in blue and mine is green. Looking at her, I'm starting to wish I'd got the blue one.

Maxie picks up our secret code. 'What's this?'

'It's—' Abby starts, but Maxie interrupts her.

'Oh, I get it,' she says. 'It's a substitution code.'

I bet they teach this stuff at her school for the gifted. The students are all probably training to be spies.

Obi steps forward. 'Yes, what you do is—'

But Maxie holds up her hand like she doesn't need any help. She grabs a piece of paper and starts decoding the message I wrote earlier.

Mates Ove . . .

I can't help myself, I snatch the paper off her. 'I'm sorry Maxie – only Mob members can see this.'

Maxie turns to me, her eyes twinkling. 'So what do I have to do to get in?' she asks.

Obi and Abby have not sensed the mood. Obi grins, and I guess she's remembering our conversation from earlier. 'You have to pass an initiation test,' she says with a giggle.

Abby giggles too. 'To prove yourself worthy.'

'Bring it on,' says Maxie.

'That's the kind of Mob spirit we like to . . .' says Obi, but a look from me makes her stop.

Me, Abby and Obi go into a huddle.

'What could we do for her initiation test?' whispers Abby, but Maxie is only a metre away from us so I'm sure she can hear. 'What could we make difficult for a brainiac?'

'We could say that she has to do all of our homework for the next month,' Obi says, thinking outside the box. 'And we have to get *A*s for everything.'

'Boring,' says Abby.

'And too easy,' I say. I know we were only saying it as a joke, but I do want my sister to prove herself worthy – at least to prove she really wants to be in this club. 'We have to make her do something that has nothing to do with being clever,' I say. 'Something cringy.'

'Great idea,' says Obi, giggling again. 'I've got one.'

We break away from the huddle and Obi clears her throat. 'OK, Mob Hopeful.'

Maxie straightens up and waits to hear her fate.

'Your Mission . . .' says Obi.

'If you choose to accept it,' adds Abby.

'Is to sneak out into the street,' Obi continues, 'and . . . show your bum!'

The three of us giggle again.

This is perfect. There is no way that Maxie would embarrass herself like that. She won't want to do it, so she can't be in the club. Then it won't seem like I am being a horrible sister.

'I have to go into the street,' repeats Maxie, clenching her teeth, 'and show my bum?'

'Yup,' I say. 'And sorry, I can't do you any favours just because you're my sister.' I hope the big smile on my face doesn't give away my true feelings.

Maxie paces up and down the length of my bedroom.

'It might be cold, remember,' I tell her.

'Er, it's August!' Obi says.

Maxie stops pacing. 'Don't worry,' she says. 'I'll do it.'

'Huh?' I cannot believe that Maxie is going to humiliate herself to get into my club. Maybe she genuinely wants to be friends. Like we used to be.

She flings open the door and her footsteps fade as she goes downstairs.

The other two haven't budged, still in shock.

I start running. 'Come on!'

We scurry down to the TV room and look out of the window. Maxie is walking past Mum's car on the front drive, then she gets to the street and stands there, not moving.

'She's not doing anything,' says Obi.

Two people walk by. Maxie must be waiting for them to pass.

'Do you think she'll do it?' Abby asks me.

'I'm not sure,' I say. 'I think she might.'

We're watching and waiting as Maxie stands there. Then she turns round and walks back into the driveway.

She didn't do it.

For some reason I feel disappointed.

We all go to the front door to let her in.

'Were you too scared?' asks Obi.

'Were there too many people?' asks Abby.

Maxie says nothing and walks past us to the bathroom, locking herself in.

I'm pretty ashamed of myself. I just tried to get my sister to embarrass herself in public.

When Dad left, it nearly killed me. Then Maxie left too, and I was torn apart. We were so close. Even though we always had separate rooms at Mum's, she would bring her duvet into my room and sleep there. She said it was to look after me, but I knew it was me looking after her. Where did all that go? A few months ago we were friends. Why has everything with my sister changed?

I lean on the door. 'Don't be upset, Max,' I say. 'We'll think of something easier. You could—'

The door opens so quickly I stumble forward, almost crashing into her. I look up to see if she's OK, to see if I've made her cry. I couldn't stand it if I made her cry.

But her face is blank.

'Done,' she says. Her expression switches from blank to smug.

I look at the other two, but they seem just as confused as I am.

'I went out into the street,' she says, pointing to the front door. 'And I showed my bum,' she says, pointing to the bathroom door. 'You never said I had to do both things at the same time.'

Great. Maxie is being a nightmare. And she's so smart there's nothing I can do about it.

Obi pulls nervously at the hair at the back of her neck.

Maxie holds her hand out. 'Can I see that code now?'

My sister has changed, and it seems like the change is permanent.

Chapter 5

Obi uses my computer to go on Facebook. She clicks the drop-down menu to start a new fan page.

'With this we can let people know about our fundraising club,' she says, 'and how they can donate.'

'Cool idea,' says Abby. 'We can advertise our events.'

'And tell them how much money we've raised,' I add.

Maxie does an exaggerated sigh. 'Oooh, a Facebook page. No one has ever thought of *that* before.'

It's still my birthday sleepover, but Maxie is not exactly part of the party. We're huddled round my laptop while she sits at my dressing table, fiddling with my stuff without asking. She must be doing it to annoy me.

'If you're not going to help us, why don't you go to your room?'

'I'm in your club, remember?' she says. 'I'll bring my duvet in here and sleep with my lovely Mob pals.'

I roll my eyes, but she pretends not to see.

'Tara, could you come here for a moment, please?' Mum calls.

'This time it *has* to be takeaway!' says Abby.

Abby and Obi shove me off my chair and out the door. Maxie doesn't even look up from curling her eyelashes.

I run down to Mum, but she's not in the kitchen, she's standing in the posh drawing room. Which is not a good sign. The drawing room is the biggest, fanciest room we've got, with huge white sofas and a large fireplace with a mantelpiece with rows of my mum's expensive ornaments on top. The ornaments are her collection of glass figurines from Venice and we're banned from going within a metre of them. Mum put a bolt on the top of the door to keep us out. Maxie and I were not allowed to play in this room when we were little. We're not allowed to play in it now. Who am I kidding? We won't be allowed to play in it when we're seventy. This room is reserved for adult dinner parties and intense conversations. This is the room where Mum and Dad told us about the divorce.

'Is everything OK, Mum?' I say. I'm looking around for a takeaway menu, but she's just holding the house phone.

Mum makes a noise that sounds like everything is absolutely not OK. 'I need to let you know . . .' she says, and I'm worried in case she's about to tell me something really, really bad. 'I've been speaking to your father,' she continues, waving the phone a little.

Definitely big news. Mum and Dad never really speak any more. When he picks us up he has to call from the end of the road.

'Maxine won't be going back to Wokingham School for the Gifted next week.'

'What? Why?'

'We just need to sort something out with the school first,' she says.

'OK . . .' I say. Oh no. Have they found out what I did?

'Your dad and I couldn't quite agree: he said we should wait until it gets sorted out, but I said we should go ahead, as an emergency, just in case they don't take her back.'

'Go ahead with what? Why wouldn't they take her back?' Maybe they are chucking her out for being an imposter. Maybe—

'It's a bit complicated,' she says. 'We'll have a clearer picture when we see Mrs Eames next week.' Mum's clenched teeth let me know she doesn't want me to ask any more questions.

But there's one thing I have to ask. 'Doesn't she have to go to school?'

Suddenly the answer is obvious. I know because of the look on Mum's face, and why she's called me in, and why's she's speaking to me in the same voice she used when my guinea pig died.

'On Monday morning Maxie's coming with you. She's going to start at Hillcrest High.'

I knew it! She'll come to Hillcrest and be better than me. I won't be special. I can't believe Maxie's stolen this.

'But doesn't she . . .?' I'm about to ask about the entrance exams, but given that she's a genius,

Hillcrest probably said she didn't have to do them.

Mum's not really listening anyway. 'She's going to be in Year 8, with you.'

As Maxie and I are the same age, we're in the same year. She's clever enough for Year 9, but Hillcrest isn't taking girls in Year 9.

The sinking feeling gets worse

'It might just be for a few days. Until we meet with the head of WSG next Thursday.'

Fingers crossed.

'You will look after her, won't you, Tara? You know Maxie isn't confident like you are.'

I want to protest, but Mum looks so unhappy.

'Of course,' I say.

Monday is just four days away. I feel sick again. This time it's got nothing to do with too much cake mix.

Chapter 6

There is a definite buzz in the air as Abby and Obi and I walk in the gates of Hillcrest High. And it's not just first-day-back buzz. The boys outnumber the girls a hundred to one and it feels like they are all looking at us. I thought the way Donna Woods used to look me up and down at Rimewood was bad . . .

I pull at my skirt, paranoid that my bum is showing.

'Where's Maxie?' asks Obi. She's slightly more relaxed than me and Abby. Her brothers go here so she knows the school a bit better. 'Shouldn't the Mob arrive together?'

'She had to come in early,' I say. 'To get her timetable and everything.'

Truth is, I was happy Maxie left before me. I'm hoping this whole Maxie-at-Hillcrest thing won't last very long – that whatever complicated stuff happened at Wokingham School for the Gifted will get sorted at the meeting on Thursday, and everything will go back to how it was: me at Mum's, Maxie at Dad's.

It's been on my mind constantly for the last three days. What's so complicated? What could need sorting out? I don't think it's about the school fees, because even though Dad doesn't get much money from his photography work, Mum earns enough.

Is it even possible to get chucked out of a school during the summer holidays?

I'm dreading that they've found out my secret . . . but I did it years ago . . . there's no way they could discover . . . could they?

'What's going on over there?' Abby pulls me out of my thoughts. She's pointing to a crowd in a corner of the playground.

I make a big show of being interested. 'Let's go find out!'

Donna and Sonia – Donna's new guide dog for the unkind – are leaning back on the fence by the sports hut, and they've gathered as many people around them as they can. Even mean, spotty Craig

Hurst and three of his cronies are there. Donna and Sonia are holding pads of paper and matching pens with fluffy creatures on the top that wobble when they move.

'. . . such an honour to be part of the 3Ms,' says Donna, who is mid-speech, 'that we think it's worth it.'

In the middle of the crowd I see Reece. How does he look so cute in his school uniform? His hair is all messy and sweet. I shove my way through and poke him in the back. 'What's the 3Ms?' I whisper.

When Reece sees it's me he smiles and I melt a little bit. 'Hi, Tara,' he says. 'It's so cool that you decided to join Hillcrest.' He raises a suspicious eyebrow. 'Did you join just because I told you to?'

He's laughing, but he has no idea how close he is to the truth. In fact, that's the *exact* truth. 'Er . . .' I can feel myself going red, but decide to style it out. 'Yup, I'm your stalker. Didn't you know?'

He laughs again.

Change the subject back. 'So, what's the 3Ms?'

'It's the name of Donna's club,' he says.

What?! I look at the other two, who have followed me over. 'What club?'

Abby does an exaggerated gasp.

'How dare she?' says Obi.

Perhaps it wasn't such a clever idea to broadcast on Facebook that we'd started a club.

'Are you joining her club?' I ask Reece. This could be a disaster. If Reece joins then he'll spend all his time with her and fall for her amazing hair.

'No,' he says. 'But I did want to ask Donna something.'

Please don't say he wants to ask her out.

'No talking at the back!' Sonia shouts.

Reece shuts his mouth quickly, like he's scared to be told off. We both laugh, but I'm desperate to find out what he wants to ask Donna.

'Hi, Tara,' I turn around to see the girl with curly blonde hair and freckles, still wearing about seventeen home-made scoobie bracelets up her arm. I search my mind for her name.

'Hi,' I say. 'Candice, isn't it?'

She nods. 'Candy. Did you hear about the *new* new girl?' she asks. 'Do you know why she didn't come to the Introduction Day? Do you know who she is?'

With all these changes in Maxie lately, who she is is a complete mystery.

'Actually she's my sister. She's only here for today. Or just a few days. She'll be going back to her old school soon.'

'Oh, really? Where did she go before? How come she's here just for today? And she's in our year? Does that mean you're twins?'

This Candy is a nosey one.

'You! Candy!' Donna points at us. 'Quiet! Or you can't be in my club.'

'That was harsh,' I whisper, keeping my voice down even though I don't want to be in Donna's stupid club.

'The 3Ms will be the best club this school has ever seen.' Donna looks right at me when she says this.

I roll my eyes back at her. 'What are you raising money for?' I call out.

Donna's fist clenches around her pretty pen.

'For Alton Towers,' Sonia replies. And everyone laughs.

Donna glares at Sonia, then turns back to the crowd. 'Umm . . . We haven't decided.' She gathers pace again. 'But if we work together we will definitely win the awesome Alton Towers trip.'

That was *totally* our idea! And it sounds as if she doesn't even care it's for charity.

'Good luck with that, losers!' shouts Craig Hurst.

His square-haircut friend says, 'Dumb girls.' And the other two snigger along.

'Also,' Donna continues, smiling at Craig to pretend she didn't hear him, 'you will have more fun and more friends and more attention from all the boys in this school.'

'I think I'll leave it,' says Reece. 'I'm not keen on attention from boys.'

I put my hand over my mouth as I giggle. His brown hair flops into his eyes and he could really use some gel. He isn't the best-looking boy in the school. He isn't even the best-looking boy in the year, but I've liked him for ages.

'See you later, Reece.' I watch him walk away.

'We are accepting male applications too!' Donna shouts after him.

It seems she wants him in her club as much as I want him to be my boyfriend. I switched schools for this. I'd die if I lost him now.

Donna's smile wavers for a second, but she carries on.

'We'll do really fun things to raise money, like make-up and hairstyling classes for those of you who desperately need help in that area.' She points out a few people in the crowd.

Abby frowns. 'What if her club gets more members than our Mob?' she hisses. 'What if they make more money?'

A few people are nodding at Donna excitedly, but some are drifting away. OK, those people are boys, probably put off by the make-up classes, but still.

'There's no way that the 3Ms will be more popular than the Mob,' I tell her. 'Donna is mean. Her club will be rubbish. None of the boys will join. No one will join.'

'Yeah!' says Obi, but she doesn't look so sure.

Craig and his cronies start to walk off too. 'One boy could raise more money than all the girls in this school put together,' he says as they leave.

'Don't count your chickens, Craig Hurst,' I say to him.

He sneers at me. 'What are *you*, Flabby Abby and Jumoke's baby sister going to do that's so brilliant?'

Abby drops her head. Obi and I round on him. Obi looks terrifying. 'If you speak to her like that again—'

'You at the back!' Everyone turns to look at us as Donna shouts. 'Either sign up, or shove off. We won't have spies from rival clubs stealing our ideas.'

Stealing her ideas! She stole *our* idea of starting a club in the first place!

'Don't worry,' I call back. 'The Mob are out of here.'

Craig and his three friends smirk at us as we go.

Behind us Donna's saying, 'Now, some of you aren't pretty enough to be in the 3Ms, so please don't be disappointed if we turn you away. But we will accept donations no matter how ugly you are . . .'

She is such a cow.

We're almost at the entrance to the main building when I hold out my arms to stop the other two. 'So what if Donna gets more people in her club?' I say. 'So what if the Mob only has three members?'

'Four members,' says Abby.

Oh yeah. Maxie.

'Four members,' I correct myself. 'As long as we raise enough money to get Becky her wheelchair, and as long as we stick to our motto – Mates Over Boys – at all times, this will be the best club ever!'

Obi and Abby start to smile.

'You're right,' says Obi. 'It's quality not quantity that counts.'

We huddle for a hug.

'Tara! Obi! Abby! Wait!'

We turn around to see Candy running to catch up with us, her blonde curls bouncing round her face.

'What's up?' I ask.

'I was . . . wondering . . .' she says, panting. 'Could I . . . join . . . your Mob?'

Did I hear her right?

'What about the 3Ms?' I say.

'Not interested,' she says. 'Donna's actually my next-door neighbour—'

'Poor you,' says Obi.

'She's too bossy,' Candy continues. 'Her club wouldn't be any fun. Apparently, 3Ms stands for *Me Me Me.*'

'There's a surprise,' I say, and we all laugh.

I give Obi an *I told you so* look, then say, 'You can be in the Mob . . .' Candy beams and looks at the other two who nod at her. 'But you have to do an initiation test . . .'

Candy braces herself.

'Make one of your scoobies for each Mob member.'

Candy beams again. 'Done!' she says.

I give Abby a mini high five. The Mob is growing!

Chapter 7

'Have a good first day today, everyone,' Mrs Martin says as the bell goes. I feel really lucky that she's my form tutor as well as the head of year. 'Don't get lost!' she adds with a chuckle.

The boys in the class scrape their chairs back and start to leave. It's OK for them – they know their way around.

Abby stares down at her timetable. 'What have you got first?' she asks me.

Abby's in my form, which is brilliant. In fact, I think Abby's parents might have asked. But what makes me feel like the luckiest girl in the world is that my sister *isn't* in my form.

'Not sure,' I say, staring at the piece of paper I have glued on to the back of my homework diary. 'I think it's Spanish. In room 29. Wherever that is.'

We pile out of the room and into the corridor. The boys stream past like cars on a motorway and it's difficult to cross without getting smashed to death.

'I'm in room 28 for Spanish,' she says. 'Do you think that means we're in different classes?'

I can't help but laugh. 'I think so, yes, Abby.'

Abby laughs too.

'What class is Reece in?' I whisper.

'There you are!' I hear Maxie's voice somewhere behind me, but I can't see her because of some boys playing keepy-uppy with a lunchbox.

'I'm here, little twin,' she says, but I still can't see.

A hand sticks up from the crowd and waves. I'm glad she's found me. Mum would kill me if I didn't look after her.

'Tara,' she yells, pushing through the boys. She's followed by Hannah and Indiana. 'I've been looking for you everywhere!' She says this so loudly everyone turns.

'Oh my god,' Indiana says. 'Maxie said she had a twin here.' She looks back and forth between the two of us. 'You two look so much alike.'

This happens all the time – people assume we're twins because we're the same age. 'No, we're not actually—'

'Ohhhh,' says Hannah, who's next to her. 'So *you're* Maxie's twin.'

How come Maxie is Little Miss Popular all of a sudden? It's only nine o'clock!

Maxie comes forward and puts her arm around me – addressing her audience. 'Yes . . . my lovely twin sister, Tara.' She plants a big kiss on my cheek. 'But *I'm* the evil twin.' Her eyes twinkle.

Everyone cracks up laughing.

'What classes have you got today, Maxie?' I ask her. 'We could try to find the rooms together.' In my mind I see Mum smiling at me.

'I doubt we'll have any of the same classes, do you?' she says.

Of course we won't. Maxie will be in the Gifted and Talented classes.

Hannah turns to me, and I'm hypnotized a little by her swinging ponytail. 'Your hair is so awesome, Tara.'

What a nice thing to say. 'Thanks, Hann—'

'I wish I had a cool sister to teach me how to do my hair nicely.'

I'm trying not to get annoyed, but Maxie only started taking an interest in this stuff four days ago. If anything, she must have picked up her tips from me.

'What's going on?' Donna has found us in the corridor. I reckon she suffers from chronic FOMO. She needs to be in the centre of things or else she comes out in a rash.

'This is my sister—' I tell her, but Maxie breaks in.

'Hi, I'm Maxie. Tara's my sister.' She bats her eyelashes and sticks out her hand.

Donna's mouth drops open and she shakes Maxie's hand awkwardly. 'I didn't know Tara had a sister.' Donna looks Maxie up and down, then plasters a big smile on her face. 'I can't believe you've been here all morning and we haven't asked you to join our club – how rude are *we*?'

All the girls start muttering, remembering how, about twenty minutes ago, Donna made it really difficult to join her club.

Sonia shifts her weight to one foot, trying to act confident as the second-in-command, but the look on her face says she knows one word from Donna could change that.

'Yes, Maxie,' says Sonia, 'you should totally be in the 3Ms. It's so worth the joining fee.'

I feel mean, but I can't help laughing.

'In fact,' Donna tells Maxie, using her sweetest voice, 'we could forget about the joining fee, just this once.'

I turn to Maxie and roll my eyes. As if she would join the *Me Me Me* Club when she already has the Mob? I mouth at her, *'It's OK – I'll tell them.'* Because I know how Maxie hates speaking to strangers.

'Actually, Donna,' I say, trying to let her down gently. 'I'm afraid—'

'Actually, Donna . . .' Maxie interrupts me. I'm kind of proud of my sister for sticking up for herself. I smile at her in an encouraging way. Weirdly, Maxie won't make eye contact.

She takes a deep breath, then turns it into a bored kind of sigh. 'Thing is, I'm already in a club.'

'Yeah,' I say. Abby, Obi, Candy and me move over to stand by Maxie. 'Maxie is in the Mob, so—'

'Actually, Tara.'

Interrupted by Maxie. *Again!* This is starting to become a habit, and one I don't like.

'Thing is,' she says, still not quite looking at me properly, 'I'm starting my own club.'

Whaaaaa . . . ?

'What?!' says Obi, managing to actually speak, unlike me.

'Yup,' says Maxie, and she starts looking at her nails as if this is normal, and not the biggest, most hurtful and humiliating thing she has ever done to me. 'A new club, and it's called: the Club.'

I can't quite believe this. The Mob are all looking at me like Maxie is my responsibility and I should be able to control her.

'That's so cool!' says Indiana.

The others start nodding in agreement.

'I definitely want to be part of the Club,' says Hannah. Then she looks a bit nervous. 'Can I join?' she asks Maxie.

'Of course,' says Maxie. She grabs her bag and whips out a sign-up sheet with cool images off the internet. To have had time to design and print this out, she must have done it over the last few days. Just after we allowed her to join the Mob.

'Er . . . just to let you know,' Donna says, 'the 3Ms have a special introductory rate – for today only.'

Everyone rolls their eyes. The look on Donna's face would make me laugh if I wasn't pretty sure I am pulling the exact same one. I'm embarrassed. I'm angry. I'm hurt.

I pull Maxie away from her adoring fans and into a Mob huddle. 'What are you doing?'

'Yeah,' says Obi, scowling. 'You're supposed to be in the Mob.'

Maxie laughs us off. 'And what? I'm in for life?'

Abby frowns too. She knows Maxie well enough that she has the right to feel hurt by this too. 'Max, you passed the initiation test. We told you our secret code. We let—'

'You didn't tell me your secret code,' Maxie says really loudly. 'I cracked it.' I can't believe Maxie is doing this to me. 'Mum said I had to join your club,' she says, and now she meets my eye, 'but now I'm at Hillcrest, I don't want to.'

'You're not even going to *be* at Hillcrest for that long!' I remind her.

She mutters something that sounds like, '*We'll see.*'

I'm fuming. But if you can't join them, beat them!

I move past her and speak to the other girls. 'You could all join the Mob instead,' I say. I decide to get rid of all the initiation tests and proving worthy stuff – unworthy members might have to do. 'There's no sign-up sheet. No joining fee. We have our own meeting room in the girls' loos and . . .' Everyone is looking at me like I'm crazy. '. . . and we're really nice,' I add quietly.

Hannah snorts with laughter. 'Why would we sign up to your club when we have a newer, better one on offer?' she says.

'Yeah,' Indiana agrees. 'I want to be in the cool twin's club.'

Now Maxie is *the cool twin*! I feel a lump rise in my throat.

'Come on, Tara,' says Abby, taking me by the arm. 'We'll be late for class.'

The corridor is almost empty.

Hannah looks at her watch, a bit worried. 'Should we go too?'

Maxie flaps her hands. 'Nah. They won't tell us off for getting lost today.'

The Mob drag me away from my sister. Candy can't tear her eyes from the other girls lining up to join Maxie's club.

'We don't need them, Candy,' Obi snaps, pulling her a little harder.

'Why would your sister betray the Mob like that?' asks Abby.

'Who cares?' says Obi. 'We don't need members who are disloyal.'

Maxie has betrayed the Mob and been a disloyal member. But it feels more like she's betrayed and been disloyal to me. She's my sister. Why can't she act like it? Why is she being so mean?

Chapter 8

We're not allowed to use our phones during school hours. But it's lunchtime, and us girls have only been at the school three days, so if I get caught I'll pretend I don't know. 'Did you put the goggles in my locker for me?' I say down the phone.

'Yup.' Abby's waiting for me in the changing room while I get my stuff.

'Thanks. I'll get them and be there in three.'

'What are you wearing?' Abby asks.

'Seeing as we're going swimming,' I say, 'I thought I'd bring my waterproof ball gown.'

'Well, *obviously* you'll wear a swimsuit,' she says. 'But what *kind*? I don't want to look stupid.'

'You wouldn't look stupid if you were standing next to me when I'm wearing my *I'm with stupid* T-shirt.'

She cracks up. 'I've brought my one-piece. Are you wearing a one-piece?' Somehow I can hear she's biting her nails. 'I don't want to look too . . . you know . . . fat.'

Swimming in the school pool at lunch break seemed like such a good idea – Rimewood didn't have a pool, so this should be fun. Now the thought of being half-naked in front of all these boys is mortifying. But Abby said she wanted to get some exercise, and as her best friend, I'm going with her. We can shake charity tins at people later. Now it's time for dutiful friend duties.

'Abby, your hair is like the silk of the gods. Your skin sparkles like the Caribbean Sea.' Abby starts to giggle. 'And you, my friend, are *not* fat. You have something to fill your bra. I could rent out space in mine!'

'Today we say, "Goodbye, Flabby Abby." '

'Don't ever say that!' I tell her. 'You are *not* Flabby Abby.'

'Thanks, Tara.'

'I hear some of the boys from Year 12 lifeguard at lunchtime,' I tell her. 'Once we've done twenty lengths, we should treat ourselves to a good drowning, then hopefully get a mouth-to-mouth session.'

'Now that's what I call motivation!'

'Won't be long,' I say.

When I get to the third-floor corridor it's empty, as most of the boys are outside playing football, or swapping trading cards. But then I catch a glimpse of some messy brown hair.

I fiddle with the lock on my locker so he doesn't catch me looking. I can feel my face has already gone red, and I need it to calm down before I say anything. What can I say that's both hilarious and brilliantly flirtatious? I unlock my lock. What about my impression of Mrs Martin?

I open my locker. My stuff pours out of it. I try to catch it all, but it comes out so fast I can only save one or two things. There is a loud clattering sound as everything I own falls on to the floor.

Good one, Tara.

I dare to look up.

Reece is looking! I lift my hand slowly and wave. My sports bra is dangling from my fingers. I have just waved my bra at the boy I fancy! Not sure if that's flirtatious. It might be hilarious . . . but not in the right way. And now my face is burning.

Wow, I am good at this.

'Hi, Tara,' he says, walking over. 'Do you need a hand?'

'Oh, you saw that?' I say.

He nods, wrinkling his nose. 'And I think everyone in the school just heard it too. Look.'

Mr Patel, who was marking books in one of the classrooms, is looking out at me and frowning.

Reece laughs. 'Come on, I'll help you. Do you need this . . .' He bends down to pick something up. When he rises again he's as red as I am. '. . . Um . . . swimming . . . bikini . . . costume . . . thing.'

He stumbles over the word *bikini* in the cutest way imaginable. Especially cute as it's not even a bikini. I take it from him and we work together in silence as he helps me put the rest of my stuff back in my locker. Then – oh no! – he has my homework diary! My homework diary which has 'RL' in a bright red heart on it!

I grab it from his hands.

'Oi!' he says. 'What's that about?'

'Nothing,' I say. But now of course he wants the homework diary. 'It's just—'

He snatches it back. 'Argh!' I scream. 'Give it!'

I try to grab it but he yanks it out of my reach.

'Reece!' I yell.

He laughs. 'What's the magic word?'

'Idiot?'

He laughs harder. 'Nope. Try, *Reece is the best*.'

'Reece is an idiot!' I yell.

'What's going on?' It's Mr Patel. He's come out of the classroom and he looks annoyed. 'Reece, give the poor girl her book back.'

Reece hands me my homework diary.

'It's OK, Mr Patel,' I say. 'We were only being silly.'

'Silliness is for the playground, not the corridor.' He shoos us away.

We run down the stairs together. 'I think we just got chucked out,' I say. 'I know I should be ashamed, given it's my first week here and everything, but actually I'm pretty proud.'

He looks proud too. 'How rock and roll are we?'

'Pretty rock and roll.' I jump off the bottom step on to the second floor, twirl round, scrunch up my eyes and do the *rock-out* hand signal. Then I think I might look stupid, but when I open my eyes again he's doing the rock-out hand signal too, and adding in some air guitar.

I join in, strumming my imaginary strings. 'Today it's getting chucked out of the top-floor corridor. Tomorrow we'll be smashing up the top-floor penthouse of a posh hotel.' I smash my guitar for good measure.

'What are you doing?' comes a voice from inside another classroom. I freeze. Reece freezes. It's his friends Joel and Lenny.

'Um . . .' I say slowly. 'We're . . . smashing . . . our . . . penthouse . . . with our guitars.'

Joel nods like this is the most normal explanation in the world. 'I getcha.' Even though Joel's school shirt is clean and his tie is neatly knotted, he still looks untidy. It's his hair – it looks like static electricity is making it stand on end, but that's normal for him. He raises an eyebrow at my guitar pose.

'Wanna join our band?' asks Lenny, who couldn't be more different from Joel. He has a perfectly coiffed quiff. The general opinion is that he's the fittest boy in Year 8.

'That's a great idea!' says Reece. 'We're holding auditions tomorrow for a vocalist.'

'Real, or *air* vocalist?' I ask.

'Ha! Real, I'm afraid.'

'You should be afraid . . . of my singing,' I tell them. 'I make screaming foxes sound tuneful.'

'Shame,' says Reece. 'Sucker Punch could do with a female singer.'

Reece wants me to be in his band. This is so, so cool!

'Are you any good?' I ask.

The boys look at each other like, *What a stupid question!*

'We're phenomenal!' says Joel, at the exact same time Reece says, 'We're rubbish,' and Lenny says, 'We're OK.'

I laugh. 'Hmm, mixed reviews. I'd love to hear you play sometime.' As soon as the words come out I worry. Did that sound desperate?

'Come now!' says Reece, glancing at his band mates as if to check it's all right. 'We're off to jam in one of the music rooms.'

I don't believe it! Reece has just asked me to hang out with him! I'm so excited, and – then it hits me: I said I'd meet Abby. 'Umm . . . sorry . . .' I say, trying not to sound as gutted as I feel. 'I have to do something.'

'Fair enough,' says Reece. He turns away from me so easily.

I text Abby.

Reece just asked me to hang out with him!!! I've said I can't but do you think he'll ever ask me again?

My phone beeps back.

OMG!!! Forget about swimming. This is much more important.

I clearly forgot that Abby is the best. My phone beeps again.

And maybe you could introduce the band to the rest of the Mobsters and we could be their official fan club. I wouldn't mind fangirling Joel. Please don't tell him that.

My first Mob Mission – to get Joel and Abby together!

'Reece! Wait!' Oh God, I'm pretty sure that was desperate. 'I'm coming,' I say, and run. And I'm *certain* that's desperate.

When I catch up with them I'm panting. 'I was meeting Abby, but it turns out she's busy.' I try to catch Joel's eye. 'She's my best friend. She's brilliant.' Joel is too engrossed with cleaning out his ear with his finger to notice.

But that's OK. Everything else might be bad – the Club has two members, Hannah and Indiana signed up straight away, so they are almost as popular as the Mob. And even though Maxie said it was a rubbish idea when we did it, the Club have started a page on Facebook too. I haven't seen them do any actual fundraising, but somehow the Club has got £43. Abby, Obi, Candy and I put in all our savings so now the Mob has £47. It's a lead, but not much of one.

And let's not forget that I have to deal with a daily overdose of Donna Woods. She only has Sonia in her 3Ms, but she still gives all the big talk about beating us.

The only girl left is that quiet girl, Simone. But she seems to be keeping out of it all.

So everything else is bad . . . but I *knew* there had to be upsides to being a girl in a boys' school! Once I start going out with Reece, Joel will get to know Abby and he'll fall for her. And maybe there will be band members for Obi and Candy too.

It's not till hours after the practice that I see another message from Abby:

There's some weird noises in the girls' changing rooms. I think someone's hiding in here. It's like I'm being watched.

Creepy! I'll have to ask her about that later. Turns out you can't even go swimming without heaping on the drama.

Chapter 9

Dad leans over and rubs Mum's back, whispering, 'It'll be OK, love,' into her ear. Mum smiles at him, even though he's not supposed to be calling her 'love' any more.

They have dragged me along to this after-school meeting with them and Maxie at Wokingham School for the Gifted. Apparently the headmistress wanted me to come too. Mum and Dad want WSG to take Maxie back, and Mum asked me to be on my best behaviour. Trouble is, I haven't been speaking to Maxie since Monday when she started at Hillcrest and announced the Club. But if it gets Maxie away from Hillcrest and living back at Dad's, I will grow an actual halo just for them.

The good news is that Dad has been over to the house almost every night after school, talking to Mum about this meeting. That hasn't happened since the divorce. Maybe all this weirdness is part of some genius plan of Maxie's to get Mum and Dad back together.

'The headmistress will be out in a moment,' the receptionist says.

Mum and Dad won't smile at Maxie though, and for a minute even I feel sorry for her. Maxie's still wearing her new look – a pretty purple top, smart blue jeans and loafers – but her nervous grungy scowl is back. I know the psychic game we play isn't real, but maybe we're semi-psychic, because I feel nervous as well. Like sick-to-my-stomach nervous. I'm afraid somehow we're here because of me, and that's why the headmistress wants me to come.

I've done something that no one knows about. Not Mum or Dad or Maxie. Not even Abby.

Of course Maxie is clever. *Really* clever. Like Einstein, Stephen Hawking, Isaac Newton clever. But while Maxie will probably design a rocket that flies to a different solar system, or invent a new kind of maths (yuck!), she can't write well. Not to save her life. I sneaked a peek at the personal statement she wrote to get into Wokingham School for the Gifted, and it was awful.

Yeah, she knows how to spell most words and how to put those words into a sentence and how to put sentences into a paragraph, but she doesn't know how to make any of it sound good. I knew there was no way she'd get a place if she submitted that.

So I might have taken Maxie's personal statement and rewritten it for her.

And Maxie got in.

And nobody knows.

Yet.

The door opens and the headteacher – Mrs Eames – pokes her head out. I was expecting someone scary, but she's wearing really unscary green corduroys and a blue woolly jumper. 'Come on in,' she says, as if she's calling her cat from outside.

'This is my younger daughter, Tara,' Mum says, introducing me, and I get up.

'Hello, Tara, thank you for coming.' She turns to my parents. 'I thought it would be good to have the whole family together for this.'

Mum stutters for a second. 'Um . . . yes . . . of course.'

'We're a very close family,' says Dad, putting his arm around Maxie.

Maxie shrugs Dad's arm off her, but Dad styles it out by yawning.

If we're trying to seem non-dysfunctional, I'm not sure we're succeeding.

Mrs Eames's office is an antique – wood panels, a portrait on the wall of an ugly headmaster from a hundred years ago, and an old-fashioned bell that must have been used to summon the butler back then – but she's done it up as nicely as she can, with funky lamps, an Apple Mac, a comfy sofa and single armchair at one side, and pictures of her family on a desk in the middle of the room.

She gestures to us to sit on the sofa and we all squeeze in together.

No one wants to speak. Mum looks at Dad, but he's saying nothing.

Eventually Mum sighs to signal she'll go first. 'We're pleased you called this meeting, Mrs Eames,' she says. 'We know we have a lot to talk about, and we know what Maxie did was wrong.'

What *did* Maxie do?

'But we really hope you'll consider letting her return.'

Please say yes please say yes please say yes.

'They have a gifted-and-talented programme in the school we've had to place her in for now, but we feel Maxie would really benefit from your world-renowned, specialist teaching.'

If I wasn't on my best behaviour I would gag over Mum's blatant butt-kissing.

'And term doesn't start here until next week,' Dad adds, 'so she won't have missed anything, will she?'

Mum and Dad look at Mrs Eames like dogs begging for a treat.

Mrs Eames turns away from them to speak to Maxie. 'We're sorry we had to let you go, Maxine,' she says. 'You were one of the most talented children at the school.'

Dad can't help but smile with pride. I have to say that I'm pretty impressed too. So Maxie is one of the *gifted* gifted people.

But then this doesn't make any sense. Why did Maxie have to leave? My heart is pounding. This is it. This is why Mrs Eames wanted me here – she knows I wrote the personal statement.

Mrs Eames turns to Mum and Dad. 'Maxie's maths abilities are outstanding,' she says.

She's not wrong. I've seen Maxie's maths homework and I don't even recognize half the symbols on the page.

'And her personal statement was one of the best we've ever had.'

I choke. *Did she just say . . . ?*

'Are you OK, Tara?' Mum asks.

'Fine,' I cough. 'I just . . .' *The best they've ever had!* I beam into my lap and wish I could tell Mum and Dad the truth. Then maybe Dad would smile as proudly for me as he just did for Maxie.

Mrs Eames ignores my coughing fit and continues. 'But Maxine's attitude started to change at the end of the last term.'

Mum looks at Maxie, then back to Mrs Eames. 'In what way?'

'She started . . .' Mrs Eames is searching for the right words. Meanwhile I'm thinking, *Best they've ever had!!!* '. . . acting up.'

'Oh?' says Mum, sounding concerned.

'Nothing serious,' Mrs Eames says, 'just being a little moody and bolshie.'

I remember when that started, I think. And, *The best they've ever had!!!!*

'We organized a school trip to visit Oxford University, and Maxie didn't want to go.'

Dad splutters. 'That's OK, isn't it? If she doesn't want to visit a university?' He's starting to sound angry and I wish he wouldn't.

'Of course it is,' says Mrs Eames, still calm. 'It's just that when Mrs Critcher asked her why, Maxie was quite rude.'

I glance at Mum. Her expression is somewhere between angry, confused and worried. 'Why didn't you want to go on the trip, darling?'

Maxie looks at the floor.

That's not enough for them to expel her though, is it? Mum and Dad clearly know what happened and I'm the only one left out.

'Let's get to the point,' Dad says. 'You say she took some money.'

I gasp. I didn't mean to – best behaviour and everything – but . . . *stealing!* Enough to get her expelled! I don't know Maxie any more. I really don't. It's not like Mum and Dad give us a million pounds a month or anything, but I get the same allowance as most people. And if I really need something I can always ask for more. What can she have wanted that cost so much? A computer? A horse? A boob job? Maybe she was planning to donate to Becky's charity?

'I mean . . .' Mum butts in, 'Maxie hasn't opened up to us about it . . . Are you even sure it was her? Who else was in the building when the money went missing?'

Mrs Eames gives her a pitying look. 'It wasn't like that,' she says. 'You see, money was transferred online out of the school's account into a personal account.'

Computer theft? They can't think it was Maxie.

'You're suggesting she hacked into the school's bank account?' says Mum, laughing because it's so ridiculous. 'How would she know how to do that? Why do you think it was her?'

'The money was transferred to *her* bank account,' Mrs Eames says. 'With her name.'

So it's true. She did it.

Mum opens her mouth again, but Mrs Eames adds, 'It was verified by both banks.'

Dad gets up and starts pacing. 'Could you not overlook it this time? Take Maxie back and put her on report or something? She's just fooling around. You know what teenagers are like.'

My sister is an internet fraudster – a cyber-hacker. A thief. But the weirdest thing about this is that Maxie must have known they would trace it back to her. If she's such a genius, why would she do something so stupid?

Mum gets all polite, backing Dad up, but overcompensating for his manic pacing. 'Maxine will repay the money,' she says. 'With whatever interest—'

Mrs Eames holds up her hand. 'Repayment is not the problem,' she says.

Mum and Dad glance at each other.

'You see,' Mrs Eames continues, 'Maxine stole 1p.'

1p?

One. Pee.

From my parents' expressions, I can tell they didn't know this, and can't work it out either. It's like stealing £1,000 is acceptable. Stealing 1p makes you crazy.

Mum has gone completely white. 'Why did you do that, darling?' she asks, her voice shaking. She wipes her cheek.

Maxie just shrugs again.

Mrs Eames lets the silence run on while we all wait for Maxie to speak. She doesn't. Mrs Eames smiles kindly. 'I wonder if I could be so bold as to suggest some counselling?'

Mum nods. Gulps away tears. Dad sits on the arm of the sofa and puts his arm around her. I have a lump in my throat. Maxie's gone crazy and everything has just got really weird.

'We'll do anything it takes to help Maxie,' Dad says.

'In fact, the reason why I asked you all in together is that I think family counselling would be best,' Mrs Eames says. 'Often you find—'

'Wait a minute,' says Dad.

'Hang on, Bill.' Mum puts her hand on Dad's knee. 'Let's hear what—'

'No!' he says, and stands up again suddenly. 'She's calling us bad parents.'

‘Please, Mr Simmons,’ says Mrs Eames, holding out her hands. ‘I don’t—’

‘I’m not sticking around to be told I need counselling,’ Dad walks towards the door. ‘There’s nothing wrong with this family!’

‘Bill, come back!’ Mum shouts at him.

He slams the door on his way out.

‘For goodness’ sake,’ Mum mutters.

Maxie purses her lips. I’m not sure if she’s trying not to laugh or trying not to cry, but I could take a good guess.

Mrs Eames does her best not to look embarrassed, but *I’m* embarrassed enough for all of us. And sort of scared, because this doesn’t make any sense. My sister stole. But she only took 1p. And it’s clearly not a genius plan to get Mum and Dad back together because Dad has stormed off and Mum’s annoyed at him. And I’m annoyed for not being told about it.

Mrs Eames is right: my family is completely mental.

The worst thing is, WSG will never take Maxie back now. I’m stuck with her.

Chapter 10

Mob HQ is looking great. We've used up one whole felt-tip pen colouring in the money-raised thermometer. After pestering our families and friends for donations, it's now at £91. Abby finished the poster – it has our star logo on it – and it's taped to the wall. We've pinned on individual photos of each Mob member – me, Abby, Obi and Candy – as well as a couple of group shots that we asked Reece to take. Then one of Reece and me that Abby insisted on taking. Cringe.

'Are you going to stop staring at that photo any time this millennium?' asks Candy.

'Was it that obvious?' I ask, pulling my gaze away.

'*Obvious?*' says Obi. 'There's drool all over the floor.'

'Er, because I'm hungry!' I say.

'Hungry for *lurve* . . .' says Obi.

There is no point in pretending. 'It's a love famine.' I sigh. 'I haven't heard from Reece since the jamming session on Wednesday. And when I was there he basically ignored me.'

Candy nods. 'Boys do take their bands very seriously.'

A thought jumps into my brain. 'OMG, I've got it! We'll throw a fundraising party. We'll charge an entrance fee and get Sucker Punch to perform!' This is one of my winning ideas!

'Then you could hang out with Reece,' says Abby. 'And I can hang out with Joel.'

I'm hit by the image of Joel picking his ear.

'Are me and Obi supposed to share Lenny?' says Candy.

'Don't worry,' I tell them. 'They held auditions for new members yesterday.'

Obi and Candy squeak at this.

'I wonder if Justin Bieber will sign up,' says Candy.

'Right, that's it,' I say. 'We're having a fundraiser party!'

To seal the deal we do the Mob secret handshake – touching palms then circling once before shaking hands properly.

'Let's start organizing.' I reach for the Mob Handbook. Abby's decorated the front of the file with the star logo and we have different sections in it: one for our attendance register, one for our accounts, one for our codes. And now I start a new section, writing 'Fundraising Party Plans' at the top, then underlining it. Then a subheading. 'Possible venues,' I say aloud. I look at Abby. 'Where should we have it?'

'How about the school gym?' Candy says.

'I don't know,' says Obi. 'It's a bit schooly.'

'But you can hire the trampoline,' says Candy.

'That *would* be cool!' I agree, writing it down and trying not to let my excitement interfere with my best neat writing. 'There would be loads of space to dance.'

'Dancing on a trampoline would be wicked!' says Abby.

I write: 'The School Gym – (perfect for trampoline dancing).'

'More important than *where*,' I say, raising an eyebrow to try to get the Mob intrigued, 'we need to think about *who*. Let's do an invitation list.'

I turn the page, then write the heading 'Guest List' and underline it with two wiggly lines.

'Obviously Mob members are VIP guests,' I say, and put our names at the top.

Abby digs a sheet of gold star stickers out of her bag and sticks one next to each of our names.

'Then . . . of course . . .' I continue.

'*Reeeeeece* . . .' they all say together, and giggle.

'Does he get a star?' Abby asks.

I shake my head. 'It's mates over boys, remember? Reece is important, but not as important as us.'

The door to the girls' loo opens. We all go silent. The sheet we've hung up is not exactly soundproof and we don't want anyone to hear our Mob business.

Obi sticks her head out beyond the sheet to take a look. 'It's Maxie,' she says, her voice coming out like a groan.

'Oh, great,' I say. I don't bother to hide the sarcasm. Maxie, the mastermind behind the Great Wokingham Heist of the Century. She's an incompetent thief or a crazy person. Either way, she's always mean to me and I don't want her anywhere near the Mob.

I stick my head round. 'Hopefully she'll just do what she's here to do and *get out*,' I say, looking straight at Maxie.

She ignores me. She's holding the door for Indiana, who follows her in.

'I heard Indiana signed up to the Club,' Abby, who's now standing next to me, whispers.

'Maybe that's it. Just Maxie and Indiana,' Abby whispers.

But I know they have Hannah too.

The door opens again: Hannah.

'She's just parading them in front of us to make us jealous,' I tell the others. 'But we're not jealous of the Club Club, or whatever it's called.'

But we're still all holding our breath, waiting to see if any more girls walk in.

'Yeah,' says Obi loudly, 'come on, let's carry on planning our awesome fundraising ideas.' We make a big show of coming back inside the meeting room and pulling the sheet across so they know we're not bothered they've arrived.

I look at the list so far. 'Well, I know who wouldn't be a VIP: Mr McAdam!' and we all laugh really loudly. Mr McAdam is the headmaster. He wears his trousers pulled up over his round belly. The thought of him partying is quite funny . . . but not as funny as we're pretending.

'Can you imagine him on the trampoline?' says Abby.

I hold my stomach to pretend it hurts from laughing, and sneak a sideways look out of the gap between the sheet and the wall. I tail off when I see who walks into the loos next. It's Sonia.

Candy gasps. She's seen too. 'Sonia's in the 3Ms. What's she doing here?'

Obi looks at me, her face worried. 'Sonia never does anything without Donna.'

And guess who walks in next.

Chapter 11

'Have the 3Ms joined forces with the Club?' hisses Candy.

The rest of us are too shocked to speak. If Maxie has Indiana, Hannah, Sonia and Donna, then she has persuaded every single girl in the whole of our year, apart from us, to be in her club. Every girl except Simone, who still doesn't talk to anyone.

'They have five members,' says Obi. 'There are only four of us.'

'Quality not quantity, remember?' I say.

The others don't look convinced.

The Club have huddled together and they're whispering, then really obviously throwing looks over at us.

'I actually feel sorry for them,' I say.

'Yeah,' says Candy. 'As if we care what they're doing.' But she carries on staring at them.

'It's quite sad really,' says Obi.

Finally their huddle breaks up and they start walking over. Candy lets out a little squeak. We all quickly turn back to what we were doing.

'We'll raise loads of money this way,' says Obi.

Donna marches straight up to the meeting room and pulls the sheet aside.

I don't look up. 'You can't come in unless you know the secret knock.'

'Whatever.' Donna goes back to the Club and they start whispering again.

This time Maxie comes over. 'If we guess your secret knock, you have to let us in, right?'

Could she guess it?

'It's only fair, I suppose,' mumbles Obi.

'Are you sure you haven't told your sister what it is?' Candy asks. 'Like, maybe when she was in the Mob.'

'She wasn't in the Mob long enough to have learned it,' I reply.

'OK,' Obi says to them, 'give it your best shot.'

'And you only get three tries,' I add.

'That's not fair,' Sonia whines.

'Don't worry, Sonia,' says Maxie. 'I only need *one* try.'

There's no way they could guess it. Maxie might know how to transfer 1p from one bank account to another, but she's not a mind-reader, no matter what our psychic game used to make people think.

She looks straight ahead as if we're not even there. She starts knocking . . .

. . . to the tune of Beyoncé's 'Single Ladies'.

Our secret knock.

How did she do that?

The Mob look at me open-mouthed.

Maxie keeps on knocking out the tune and I guess it's pretty obvious from our faces that she got it right. Donna and Maxie share a smug look while the other girls start singing along.

'♫ *All the single ladies. All the single ladies.* ♫'

Indiana and Hannah even start doing the dance around the girls' loos, clapping out the rhythm as they do.

'Did you tell her?' asks Abby.

'No,' I protest.

'Are you sure?' asks Obi.

'*Yes!* I definitely didn't!' I yell.

'Candy, did you tell Donna? She lives next door to you, after all.'

Candy shakes her head.

'Come on then,' says Maxie, pushing the sheet aside and barging in. 'Make room for us.'

'How did you . . . ?'

But nothing Maxie does surprises me any more.

She smiles with narrowed eyes, taps her nose, then sits on the large pipe at the back.

Donna pushes in front of the others and walks in too. She looks at our poster and photos on the wall, then turns back to Sonia and mouths, '*Lame*.'

Sonia sees the thermometer and laughs. '£91? We've got almost twice that.'

Sonia, Hannah and Indiana crowd in, shoving aside the upside-down box table to make room. Mob HQ has always been a perfect size for us; now it's tiny and suddenly feels like a toilet cubicle.

'Who told you our knock?' I say, standing up to face Maxie.

'You did,' she says.

But I know I didn't.

'All of you,' she says. 'Every time you lot walk out of this toilet you are all singing that song. *Every* time.'

Oh God. The tune *is* always stuck in my head these days.

'It's amazing how much the unconscious mind gives away,' she says, showing off to the Club. They nod seriously as if this is something they already knew.

Why can't I have a normal, non-genius sister? One that pouts and slams doors. Why do I have to have a sister that crack codes and steals irrelevant amounts of money?

'Well, whatever,' I say. 'This is Mob HQ. It belongs to us.'

The Club look to Maxie for an answer.

'Where does it say that?' Maxie asks. 'Have you rented the leasehold off the school board? Is this some ancient right I don't know about? If so, I'd like to see your papers.'

She's trying to sound like a lawyer, but she just sounds like a cow.

'We've got a poster,' says Abby quietly.

Our poster does say 'Keep Out' but I'm not sure it's legally binding.

Donna snorts. 'Play nice, won't you, children?'

I give Maxie one long look to let her know I'm not happy, but she just smiles sweetly. 'Fine,' I say. I turn my back on her and sit down opposite Candy.

'Yeah,' says Obi, 'if you don't mind us hearing your money-raising plans, that's fine.'

The Club climb over us and form their own circle at the back of the cubicle. Maxie and Donna are up against the wall, perching on the large pipe. Sonia, Hannah and Indiana sit on the floor facing them. They are so close that my back is almost touching Indiana's back – if we were friends we could lean against each other. Candy can't take her eyes off Donna.

'So, we're decided?' Maxie says to the Club. 'We're raising money for the World Wildlife Fund?'

They nod.

'Not the World Wrestling Federation,' says Donna, laughing like a donkey at her own joke. The Club joins in. It's not even funny!

'Let's carry on planning,' I say, tuning out the Club, 'because I have a new idea. Pass me the handbook.'

'I think we should start a handbook,' Maxie says really loudly.

Even though she's behind me, I can tell it's Donna sniggering. 'Yeah, we can use *our* handbook to plan our next charity event,' she says.

I turn round and glare at them. 'Stop copying us!'

'We're not,' Maxie says. She puts her hand over her heart, all innocent.

'Yeah,' says Donna, 'a club handbook is essential.' She sneers at our handbook. 'Though we'll have to make sure ours actually looks stylish.'

I feel my shoulders tensing.

All the Club members start talking really loudly.

'We could raise money by selling stuff,' says Hannah.

I roll my eyes. '*Selling stuff*,' I say. 'Why didn't we think of that?'

The Mob starts giggling. We've already planned to do a cake sale on Monday, so we're not worried.

'Selling food would raise loads of money . . . With the number of piggies who go to this school.' Donna looks across at Abby when she says this.

'Shut up!' I tell her. Then I shake my head and say loudly to the Mob, 'Let them shout over us. If they can't hear our ideas, they can't steal them.'

The Mob aren't speaking. But I'm not scared. In fact, I actually want the Club to know how much better we are than them. 'I have a brilliant plan: we should hire out BOULEVARD NIGHTCLUB.' I shout those last words.

The Club goes quiet, shocked by our amazing creativity. Maxie might have more members, but we have better ideas. We'll see who wins in the end.

'I'll call the manager and see if we can have it in a couple of weeks,' I say.

'There is no way you could hire a nightclub,' says Maxie. 'You're underage.'

'Yeah,' says Donna. 'What a stupid idea.'

'Yeah. Stupid,' Sonia repeats.

I look Maxie straight in the eye. 'We'll hire the whole place so it won't matter that we're under eighteen.'

The Mob starts a circle of secret handshakes. 'That's such a cool idea!' says Obi.

If I wanted, I reckon I could push the Club over like dominoes.

'Now,' I say, whispering, but really loudly, 'let's write down who we would like to snog at the party.'

I write 'Reece Lee'.

'Ahhhhh,' says the Mob.

'You two would make a brilliant couple,' says Abby.

The Club are listening in and I have to say I am happy to have won this round.

'We have to write down who we fancy!' shouts Donna. 'That's the most important thing.'

The Club hum in agreement with her.

'Mimicry is the highest form of flattery,' says Abby.

'I'll go first,' says Donna.

'Who would you like to snog, Obi?' I ask.

'I fancy . . .' says Donna.

'Well,' says Obi. 'I would like to—'

'. . . Reece Lee,' finishes Donna.

What?!

I glare at her. 'You do not fancy Reece.'

'Yes I do,' Donna says. 'I've liked him for ages.'

My head's spinning. She *can't* like him. What if he likes her back? I feel sick.

Then I remember what the Mob's motto is: Mates Over Boys. Donna might not be my mate, but we shouldn't fight over a boy. 'Fine,' I say. 'Let the best woman win. No hard feelings.' I stretch out my hand, waiting for her to shake it, knowing that if Donna and Reece did get together, I would find it almost impossible to keep my feelings anything less than granite.

'That's very sweet of you, Tara.' Donna leaves my hand hanging. 'But I feel like I have an unfair advantage.' She flips her hair.

'Your hair isn't irresistible, you know,' says Obi.

Donna does a long, fake laugh. 'It *is* irresistible,' she says, 'but that's not what I mean. You see' – she pauses for dramatic effect – 'I'm the new vocalist in Sucker Punch.'

I feel like *I've* been Sucker Punched. 'What?'

Donna might be a cow, but she's got an amazing singing voice. She won the talent competition at Rimewood three years in a row.

'Yup,' she says, and flips her hair again. 'Reece asked me personally to audition.'

That must have been what he wanted to ask her.

'You can't have.'

'How did you get in?'

'Did anyone else try out?'

I'm not saying these things, it's the Mob. I can't speak.

'Would you mind keeping out of the Club's business,' says Sonia. 'Why don't you mind your own?'

I look at Maxie and shake my head. 'You . . .' But I don't know how to finish that sentence. I turn back to the Mob. 'Come on, I'm calling pest control. This cubicle needs fumigating.'

Maxie sticks out her tongue.

The Mob get up and follow me, and we all leave. The Club waste no time jumping into our places on the cushions.

Maxie's out to get me at school *and* at home. The Club are battling to win the charity competition, they're fighting to get more members, they've raised more money than us, they've crashed our

Mob HQ, and now they're competing for Reece too.

Well, I'm not going to take it any more.

If it's a war they want, it's a war they're going to get.

Bring. It. On.

Chapter 12

It's 7.30 a.m. and I haven't been up this early in ages. I've definitely *never* been up, dressed and heading to school this early. Abby and I baked so much food over the weekend that we had to pack a wheelie suitcase to carry it all.

'Did you try any of the cookies after I left?' I ask her.

'No,' she says.

'Are you sure? They're pretty irresis—'

'I said no, all right!' she snaps.

'Okaaaaay,' I say, holding my hands up in surrender. I can't blame her being irritable – it *is* stupid o'clock in the morning.

Obi and Candy are already waiting for us on the corner, as planned. Each of them is carrying a cake tin.

'Morning, Mobsters,' I call.

Candy smiles. Obi frowns. 'How can you be cheerful at this hour?' she says. 'There should be a law against it.'

'Not you too,' I say. 'Abby practically bit my head off a moment ago.'

'Perhaps she's hungry,' Candy says.

'Hey!' says Abby.

'Joke!' says Candy.

There's an awkward silence.

'Sorry, Abby,' says Candy.

We start walking towards school. On Friday I had to speak to the caretaker to ask him what time the gates would be open, and whether he would set up a table for us to put our cakes on.

'Did your sister see you sneaking out this morning?' asks Obi.

'No,' I say. 'And we baked all the cakes at Abby's house so Maxie has no idea. When I got home last night she was sulking in her room, on the phone to Donna.'

'Speaking of Donna,' says Candy. 'I swear when my alarm clock went off this morning I heard her whining at her dad, and her dad's car leaving the driveway.'

There's no way Donna would be awake at this ungodly hour. Candy's hallucinating through lack of sleep.

'I'm so hungry,' says Obi. 'I swear I can smell bacon.'

'Early starts deserve a fry-up,' I say.

'I can smell it too . . .' says Abby.

We round the school gates and the aroma is overpowering. So is the noise. Which is weird, because no one should be here.

Then we see them.

'What are they doing?' gasps Obi.

The Club have set up a long table by the school entrance . . . right where we were planning to put our cake sale! Mr Armond – the caretaker – is there, and he seems to be helping them.

'Traitor,' I mutter. At least there is another table beside their one, presumably for us.

'Have they brought a TV?' Abby says.

As we get closer I can see that the Club are all there. All of them looking neat and tidy in their uniforms. And it's not a TV on their table, it's a microwave. So *this* is why I didn't see Maxie this morning: she had already left! And Candy wasn't hallucinating; Donna's dad must have brought the microwave in his car.

'Lovely morning, isn't it?' says Maxie, smiling brightly.

'What are you doing here?' asks Abby.

'Free country, isn't it?' says Donna.

'A cake sale was *our* idea,' I say, pulling my suitcase over to the table next to them.

'And it was a very good idea . . .' says Donna in a babyish voice, 'for a bunch of *losers*.'

'But we thought of a better one,' adds Maxie.

Sonia starts giggling as she pulls out a bumper bag of soft bread rolls.

'What are you selling?' I ask, but the smell of bacon, the rolls, and the bottles of ketchup and brown sauce have given the game away.

Donna leans over and whispers loudly to Maxie. 'When you two were in your mum's tum you must have got every brain cell that was meant for Tara.'

The Club start sniggering.

'We're *not* twins!' I yell.

But they ignore me.

I start unpacking the boxes. Abby, Obi and Candy join me, laying out the cakes and biscuits. It all looks, really pretty. But as the boys start arriving and I see their scruffy Monday-morning faces I realize that *really pretty* is possibly not the angle we should have gone for. These are *boys*. When it comes to food, they don't care about pretty. As a queue starts to form around the Club's table of bacon sandwiches I get the sense they might have won this round.

Craig Hurst and his friends – square-head Phil Horner, Mo Hussain and Matt Higgins – ignore the queuing system and push to the front.

'What are the girlies up to now?' Craig says.

Abby cowers a little so I step forward. 'A cake sale.'

He smirks. 'Pretty daring of you to have a cake sale when you've got Flabby Abby in your group.'

Abby bites her lip and looks to the floor.

'Don't call her that!' I say.

'She knows I'm joking, right, Abs?' he says, smiling at her.

'Right,' she says, and forces herself to laugh. 'Good one.'

I hate it when Abby doesn't stand up for herself. I want to punch Craig's lights out, but I reckon he'd punch back. 'Either buy something or bug off,' I say.

'I thought ladies were supposed to be polite,' he says.

'You thought wrong, fartface.'

Everyone laughs at that, even Mo, Phil and Matt.

Craig scowls harder. 'I'm not buying any of your disgusting-looking cakes. Why would I give you money to win the Alton Towers trip when *I'm* going to win it?'

'It's not about winning, it's about raising money for charity,' I say. But I'm pleased to see him walk away. Hopefully he'll bother the Club for their bacon sandwiches and leave us alone.

'Are you all right?' I ask Abby.

She nods. 'I'm fine.' But she doesn't look fine.

'Don't know how he expects to win,' I say, staring at the back of his spotty head. 'I've never seen him so much as shake a tin, let alone arrange an event. So unless he knows a millionaire—'

'Just forget about him,' says Abby. 'I have.'

Reecce walks over and stands between both tables. 'Wow,' he says, taking it all in. 'This looks amazing. Shame I've already had breakfast.'

'That's OK,' I say, stepping out from behind the table. 'Because this is Breakfast Dessert. It's a new thing.'

'Ingenious,' he says. He starts looking over all our cakes and cookies and I turn to stick my tongue out at Donna.

She scowls at me, and then turns her back. I hear their microwave beeping, reheating the bacon for a sandwich.

'Come on, Reece,' she says. 'You know you want to.'

Reece looks up from the cakes, looks at Donna, and then his gaze drops to her hands and the open bacon sandwich she's offering him. I hope it's the bacon that's causing his drooling, and not the girl holding it.

'We have practice today, don't we?' she says, raising her eyebrows. 'You're going to need your strength. Ketchup?'

Reece cringes. 'I do burn calories when I'm rocking out.' He grabs the bacon sandwich and hands Donna the money. 'Sorry Tara,' he says, and drops his change into my money box: 5p. Sweet of him, but hardly going to make a difference.

There is only £3.30 in the box. Now £3.35. Looking over at the Club's cash box I see they have loads more than us. They even have a ten-pound note.

'This is rubb—' I turn to say to Abby, but I stop short when I see Craig munching one of our cakes. 'Hey! Did he pay for that?'

Craig gives me an evil stare. 'Of course I did,' he says. He looks at Abby. 'Ask her.'

Abby nods. 'He gave the money to me.'

Oh. Now I feel a bit bad for calling him a thief. 'Sorry.'

'All for a good cause, innit?' he says with a smirk.

'That's the spirit,' I mutter.

I wish Abby had refused to sell him a cake, but he's only, like, the fifth person to have bought one so there's no way we could turn down his money.

I take another look at our pathetic money box. Hang on. It still has £3.35 in it.

'He didn't pay!' I step around the table.

‘I gave the money to Fla— to Abby.’

Abby looks a little startled, then starts fishing around in the pocket of her blazer. ‘Sorry, no. Yes. That was my fault,’ she says, and pulls out £1.50, which she drops into the box. ‘I accidently put his money in my pocket.’

I frown at her.

‘Just a habit thing, you know?’ she says.

I suppose. But if that’s true, then why does she look so guilty?

Chapter 13

When Obi, Candy and I get to the meeting room at lunch, Abby's already there counting our takings.

'Oh, good, you're here,' I say. 'By the time we count the money, and we factor in eating, we might be left with no time for Gorgeous Guy Safari.' I make binoculars with my fingers.

'I've already eaten my lunch,' Abby says.

'What? In here?' Obi looks a little horrified.

Which embarrasses Abby. 'It's OK,' she says.

I pull the sheet across the meeting room and nod at the cash.

'How much?' I ask, wincing a little because I'm afraid to hear the answer.

Abby puts the last of the coins into a stack and counts the stacks: '£36.45.'

'Not bad in the end,' I say. But it's nowhere near what we had hoped for.

'Add it to what we've got and we're at . . . £166,' says Obi.

Abby gets out her pens and starts colouring in the fundraising thermometer. 'The Club had £178 . . . and that was *before* the bacon sandwiches.'

'*So* not worth waking up at 5 a.m. for,' groans Candy, helping Abby with the colouring.

'What I want to know,' says Obi, 'is how the Club knew we were doing an early-morning cake sale.'

Obi's right. I was thinking the same thing.

'It could have just been a coincidence,' says Candy, shifting position on her cushion.

'It could have . . .' I say. 'But it's a pretty big coincidence . . .' I let that hang in the air for a minute. 'Did any of you say something?'

Obi looks at me as if I'm talking Martian. Abby is looking at Candy accusingly. Candy can't look anywhere but the floor and is blushing so hard she could heat the whole school.

'You didn't tell Donna, did you?' I ask her.

She shakes her head, and starts giggling in an over-the-top way. 'Isn't it funny how you feel guilty when someone accuses you of something, even when you know you're innocent?'

Obi folds her arms across her chest. 'Not really.'

'Aaaaaaanyway,' says Abby. She pulls the handbook out of her bag and opens it up. 'Back to Mob business: how's the party planning going?'

'We're all on track,' I tell her. 'Now that Donna's in Sucker Punch, we can't use the band – she'll sabotage it. But a DJ is probably better anyway.'

'Why?' asks Candy.

'It means the target – i.e. Reece – will be on the dance floor, rather than onstage. That's closer range . . . to my lips.'

The girls giggle.

This weekend we gave ourselves Mob Solo Missions: mine was to speak to the manager of the nightclub. She was really nice about us being underage, and said because it was a charity thing all they needed to secure the venue was a £200 deposit. And my mum was really cool about it and gave me the money as her contribution to the charity.

'Show them the flyer, Abby,' I tell her. Designing it was Abby's Mission, as she's the design guru.

'It's just a first draft.' She pulls it out of her bag, looking nervous.

I don't know what she's worrying about. Her design is like a proper advert for a proper nightclub night. She's done it on the computer and it has a purple background and silhouetted images of two girls dancing back-to-back. The Mob star symbol is up in the corner.

'I called it *Act Your Age*,' she says, pointing to the title in graffiti writing. 'But we can change it. What do you think?'

'Errr-maze-ing,' says Obi. We all give each other a celebratory Mob handshake.

'There's only one thing missing. Or am I being stupid?' asks Candy.

I have no idea what she's talking about so I have no idea if she's being stupid.

'The date?' Candy says.

'Oh yeah,' Abby says, 'the date. I wanted to double-check the nightclub was booked first. Are we good to go, Tara?'

'My mum gave me the money and I gave it to Dad to give to the manager yesterday.' I grab my phone out of my bag. 'I'll just give him a call.'

That's the cool thing about Dad – because he works as a freelance photographer he's always available. Mum never picks up if she's in a meeting or talking to clients or on a work trip. Which can be annoying if it's a mother–daughter emergency.

'Hi, sweetie,' says Dad. 'Everything OK?'

'Yup. I just need to check something with you.'

'Are you allowed to call me from school?' he asks.

'Not really,' I say, 'but it's important.'

Dad *hmms*. 'Really important, or *Tara* important?'

'How rude!' I say. 'It's for charity.'

Dad laughs. 'Sorry.'

'Just wanted to know if it all went OK with the nightclub people,' I say. 'Did you get the deposit to the manager?'

'Yes,' he says, 'no problem.' It sounds as if he's moved the phone away from his face.

'So it's all sorted for a week on Friday?'

'Yup. Definitely. All sorted. Stop worrying. Now get off the phone before a teacher catches you, throws you in detention and locks you away from all those boys.'

Now I laugh. 'Thanks, Dad.'

I give my friends the thumbs-up. 'It's on like Donkey Kong,' I tell them, and they grin back at me.

Abby leans on our cardboard-box table and writes the date of the nightclub night on the flyer. 'It would go there, and . . . Is that someone's phone?'

We all go quiet. It sounds like a ringtone, but really far away.

It's not mine. And from the way the rest of the Mob are looking at each other, it's no one else's either.

'Hello!' I shout. 'Is there someone here?' I wouldn't put it past the Club to have snuck in. Although my sister is bound to be more devious . . .

Speaking of my sister . . . That's *her* ringtone.

It's the old grunge band she used to like before she started liking my music.

The ringing stops. But if my suspicions are correct . . .

My phone is still in my hand and I call my sister. Instantly the ringtone starts playing again.

'How did you do that?' says Candy.

'Where's it coming from?' I ask.

We all get up and start following the noise, sniffing around for it like dogs picking up a scent.

It's coming from up high – and when I look I see an air vent above a pipe in our little Mob HQ.

'Give me a leg-up,' I say to the girls. They see where I'm looking, then gather round me, making their hands into steps for me to climb.

I whack the vent, and – just as I suspected it would – it flaps open. 'A little higher,' I say. 'I think we've found it.'

They hoist me up and I'm seething with anger because I know what I am going to find – betrayal! My stupid smart sister using her genius powers to get one over on me. I push the vent open again, reach in and my hand lands on a phone.

'Got it,' I say.

It's on voice recording. It's still going. And it's been recording for the past seven minutes and thirty-eight seconds.

'Look what she's done!' I show them the phone.

'That is so wrong,' says Candy.

I shut it off. I'm about to smash it on the floor when Obi sticks out her hand.

'Wait!' she shouts. 'We can see what else she knows.'

Obi's good. Luckily I'm able to restrain myself.

'I'm not sure we should . . .' says Candy.

I look at her as if she's crazy.

'We might not like what we hear,' she says in a small voice.

This isn't like Candy, whose nose is normally wedged firmly into everyone else's business.

I shake my head at her, tapping at Maxie's phone to get to the list of recordings. By the looks of it, she recorded us at lunch and break the whole of last week. I press play and listen to the first one:

'*Testing, testing.*' It's Maxie's voice, whispering. '*Tuesday 5 September – break time.*' There are some clunking noises, then silence. Thirty seconds later we hear Candy and Obi chatting about Lenny Fulton.

'No wonder they knew about the cake sale,' says Abby.

'That evil . . .' Obi trails off and glances at me. 'Sorry, I know she's your sister.'

'My sister's a cow,' I say.

'Agreed,' says Abby. Abby is allowed to insult my sister – she's practically her sister too. Then her face falls.

'What?'

Abby bites her lip, and whispers as if we are still being spied on. 'We've stopped the recording. She's going to know we know.'

'Good!' I say. 'I want her to know! That way she'll know why I am shouting at her so hard her hair shrivels up.'

Candy laughs. I think she's nervous.

Abby sighs. 'But that would bring the war with the Club to a whole new level. They know what we're doing. We know they know. They'll know we know they know. It's going to make this whole thing a real battle . . . and things are hard enough at this school already.'

'What do you mean?' asks Candy.

But suddenly I have an idea. 'Abby, you're brilliant!'

From the expression on her face, I can tell Abby has no idea why she's brilliant. 'What? For the flyer?'

'No, not for the flyer!' I give her a whack on the arm. 'We can use this recording thing to our advantage. If they don't know we know they know, we can feed them misinformation.'

'Oooh,' says Obi, 'just like the Allies did to the Nazis in World War Two.'

'This is revenge,' I tell them. 'This is serious. This is for our pride and dignity.'

'I thought it was for a trip to Alton Towers,' says Candy, and the others laugh.

I do not laugh. This is no laughing matter. My sister's been out to get me for a while now – I've given up trying to work out why – but I am not taking it any more. 'We're going to have to rerecord this break all over again,' I tell them. 'But this time we're going to come up with the worst plans ever.'

I see the expressions change as one by one they work out my trick.

Obi does an evil-genius laugh – 'Mwah ha ha!' – and rubs her hands together. 'I love it.'

'Anyone got any really good, really bad ideas to raise money?'

'Tons!' says Candy.

'OK, when I press record, we have to start as if we've just walked in.'

They nod.

I put my finger to my lips, press record and repeat Maxie's phrase: 'Testing, testing. Monday

11 September – break time.' I've always been annoyed when people mistake me for my sister on the phone. Finally I've found a use for it: subterfuge.

I see she has two missed calls. One from me, just now. One from Dad. He must have hung up on me and phoned her right away.

'Oh, hi, Mobsters. I see we're all here for our break-time meeting,' Candy yells, not a very subtle actress. But I know this will work – the Club are too arrogant to guess we might be on to them.

'Yes,' I say, 'and I have a berrrrr-illiant idea for raising money.'

The Mob and I giggle silently, hands over our mouths.

Watch out, Maxie. You're not as smart as you think you are.

Chapter 14

The next day I'm so excited to see if the Club have fallen for our trap that I run all the way to school. They are there, in the same place they were yesterday, but today there's no bacon-sandwich smell in the air. Just a groan of disappointment from each boy as they arrive at Hillcrest.

I run over to Abby and we do our Mob handshake.

'Not got any cakes today?' sneers Craig when he sees us.

'None of your business.' We've got enough competition against the Club. I'm not going to let Craig steal our ideas too. 'How are *you* planning to make money?'

He smirks. 'I have my ways.' And with that cryptic answer, he runs off.

'Weirdo,' I mutter.

'Please don't wind him up, Tara,' says Abby.

'I'm not scared of him,' I say, 'and neither should you be. Boys like that are all talk.' Then I spy Reece and Joel coming towards us. 'But boys like *that* . . .'

Abby starts smoothing down her hair. 'Introduce me,' she whispers.

'Hi, Reece. Hi, Joel. Hey, Joel, do you know my best friend, Abby?' I turn to Abby and she has gone bright red. She's pouting, but not very well, and she looks like a fish – a red snapper maybe. Not her best look.

'Hurrum . . . He . . . Hi,' she says.

Good one, Abby.

'You hang round the pool, don't you?' Joel says to her. I forgot Abby went swimming from time to time. Who knew that Joel knew that? Maybe he's been watching her. Maybe this will be the easiest set-up ever.

'Yeah . . .' she says.

'Are you going out with Craig Hurst?' he asks her.

If I was drinking something, it would have spurted out of my nose right now.

'Er . . . no!' I say for her.

'Oh, I've just seen you talking,' he says, going a bit red now too, 'and I thought—'

I'm incredulous. 'You must be mistaking her for some other beautiful, intelligent, wonderful girl. But wait, there is no one as wonderful as Abby! She's the absolute—'

Abby whacks me.

'Ow,' I say. 'She's a proper lady too.'

'So I see,' he says.

'Anyway,' Reece says, 'what's the deal?' He looks over at the Club. 'I got here early, desperate for Breakfast Dessert. But . . .'

'But . . . ?' But I know exactly what the deal is. We walk nearer the table – the same table that was there yesterday morning – and take a look.

'See,' says Reece, 'no cakes and . . .'

'And . . . ?' I ask, raising a gleeful eyebrow.

'And your sister's lot have got . . . porridge.' He pulls a face to show how disgusted he is. 'And when I told them I didn't like porridge, they said there was fruit.

'*Fruit!*' says Joel. 'What's that about?'

'I have absolutely no idea,' I say. Abby and I shrug innocently to the boys, but smile wicked grins at each other.

Yesterday, when we knew we were being recorded, we had Obi say that her older brothers were worried about football training, and that all these cakes and bacon sandwiches were making them tired. She said that her brother said he'd prefer a healthy breakfast. Then we planned in detail all the yuckiest, healthiest breakfasts we could think of. Including porridge. Made with water. And it looks like the Club fell for it.

The Club look awful. Even Donna hasn't washed or curled her hair this morning.

'Where have you been?' she says to us, hands on her hips.

'We're not late for registration, are we?' I do my best to look as guilt-free as their healthy snacks.

'You were supposed to be selling food again today,' Sonia says.

Donna glares at her and Sonia instantly closes her mouth.

'You know,' Donna quickly fills in, 'because you were selling food here yesterday. It was our logical conclusion.'

I have to stop myself from rolling my eyes. 'Nah,' I say, 'we were *going* to do that, but then we decided we'd raised so much money we deserved a day off.'

Abby gives a delighted hoot. 'Yep. We have something else planned.'

Sonia leans over Donna to see what I'm holding. Donna glares at her again so Sonia straightens up.

'Mind if we hand out our flyers here?' I say. 'Go on, take one.'

Because of Donna's FOMO affliction she can't help herself, and they both take a flyer. Donna even lets out a little yelp. Which catches Maxie's attention and she comes over. She grabs the flyer from Donna. Then she stares at it for ages, flipping it over to see the back, like she's checking it's real.

'So the nightclub thing is actually happening?' asks Maxie.

'Didn't I tell you she was smart?' I say to Abby, who laughs.

I know I shouldn't, but I can't help gloating. 'Normally we arrange all our plans in our meeting room – I mean, that's what it's for, right?' I allow myself a smug grin. 'But then I had this weird, spooky feeling, as if we were being watched . . .'

Sonia looks at Maxie with wide eyes. Donna, who is slightly more subtle, frowns. Maxie clenches her teeth.

'The Mob finalized all the nightclub arrangements last night,' I finish.

Abby pulls out a poster from her bag and unrolls it for the Club to see. 'And Mrs Martin said we could put this up on the noticeboard,' Abby says. The poster is similar to the flyers, but much bigger. 'What do you think?'

From the way Maxie blinks, closing her eyes for a little too long, I know she's angry. She reaches for her bag, gets her phone and starts tapping at it.

'Check your photos,' I tell her. I peer over her shoulder as she looks. 'There's a really pretty one of me.'

The gallery on Maxie's phone shows me, Obi and Candy in the meeting room. Abby took it. Our arms are round each other and we're pouting at the camera. We decided to let her know we know after all.

'And here's a lovely one of the whole Mob!' This one is a selfie of all of us that I took at arm's length. We're beaming. 'Look at how happy we are,' I say to Maxie. 'Would you send me a copy?'

She scowls and I love it.

'You can't hand out your flyers here,' she says. 'You'll disturb our customers.'

I look around. 'You're right, sorry,' I say. 'I don't want to stop *all these people* getting to your food. You might not sell anything.'

Abby and I turn and walk into school, giving each other a Mob handshake as we do. The Club's reign of terror is over. The Mob is back on top!

Chapter 15

Obi and I took the risk that the Club hadn't somehow bugged our phones and made a new plan last night. All the boys seem to be into trading cards at the moment, so we dreamed up a trading-card forum: a place where everyone can swap cards, buy sweets and drinks, and listen to cool music at the same time.

So how come Room 14 is empty?

Well, empty aside from the mountain of sweets and drinks we're supposed to be selling . . . but there's no one to sell to.

'We might as well have one,' I say to the Mob, picking up a tub of jelly rings and handing them round. 'Looks like no one is coming.'

'Might as well have them all,' says Obi, grabbing a handful and popping a Tangfastic into her mouth.

I offer one to Abby, but she shakes her head and moves away from the sweets. 'No, thanks. I'm not your waste-disposal woman,' she says.

'Well, I will,' says Candy.

I don't understand it. Obi assured us her brothers live for trading cards, constantly online buying and plotting their swaps. We researched the most popular kinds and even bought some of our own using a bit of the charity fund. Now we're back at £125. According to their Facebook page, the Club have raised £208 so far. '*Speculate to accumulate*,' I'd said to the others. It's something Dad says whenever we play Monopoly and he spends all his money on hotels. But thinking about it now, Dad always loses in Monopoly. Maxie always wins.

'If your brothers thought this was such a good idea,' Abby snaps, 'why aren't they here?'

Obi starts pulling at the hair at the back of her neck.

'It's not Obi's fault, Abs,' I say. 'We *all* thought this would be a good idea. It *is* a good idea.'

'Then where the hell are they?' Abby asks huffily.

Obi gets dialling.

I walk over to Abby and put my arm around her. I wonder if she's OK – I have been neglecting her a bit recently, what with starting a new school, obsessing over Reece and wondering why Maxie hacked into a bank to steal 1p. We haven't had a lot of BFF time.

'Is everything OK?' I ask her.

She gives an unconvincing *I'm OK* nod.

'Jumoke, where are you?' says Obi down the phone. 'I told you Room 14.'

'How's your sister?' I ask Abby.

Ever since I've known Abby – which is forever – her sister Becky has been ill. We worry about her a lot. But I've been worrying about myself a little too much recently to remember to ask. What kind of useless friend am I?

'It's not Becky,' she says, 'it's . . .' She presses her lips together.

'What?' I ask.

'You're *where*?!' shouts Obi.

We turn round.

'Some brother you are!' She ends the call. If she were a cartoon character, she'd have smoke coming out of her ears right now.

'You will not believe what they've done,' she says.

'Who?' Abby, Candy and I ask at the same time.

'The Club,' she says, and storms out of the room.

Who else?

Room 24 is heaving with people – practically the whole school is packed inside. The desks have been pulled into fours and each group of four desks is set up like one of those poker tables I've seen on TV, with boys gathered round, and a member of the Club manning each one, like croupiers. This place looks like Vegas.

I walk closer to see what they're selling. But they aren't selling, they're *trading*.

'I guess when you have a good idea,' says Abby, 'other people come up with something similar.' This line is about as believable as her *I'm OK* nod from five minutes ago.

The boys are trading so intently that a naked supermodel could walk in and they wouldn't notice. They are sizing up each other's cards, nodding, shaking their heads, swapping and turning them down.

Darnell Wade in Year 10 is trying to make a deal with Craig Hurst. 'I'll give you Wayne Rooney *and* Frank Lampard for Gareth Bale,' Darnell says.

'Throw in another one – a five-star player,' Craig says, 'or I'm walking.'

'Fine. Walk,' Darnell says, but as soon as Craig starts to go Darnell sighs, taps him on the shoulder, passes over three cards and holds his hand out.

'How do the Club *still* know everything we are about to do before we do it?' Candy whispers beside me.

'I have no idea,' I say. But somehow I just know this is Maxie's doing. And Maxie is my sister, so in a weird way that makes it my fault. Like Candy says, you can feel guilty when you've done nothing wrong.

I see Maxie in the middle of the room and push through the crowds of boys to get to her.

'Trading-card forum. Nice idea,' I say, nodding as if appraising the room. 'Shame it was *our* idea!'

Maxie smiles at me, batting her eyelashes, the same way I did yesterday over her porridge. 'Ah, my dear twin. How are you?'

'And stop calling me that!' I tell her. 'I'm *not* your twin. I would never do anything like this to you.'

Maxie's face drops. 'Sure you wouldn't,' she says. 'You're so special.'

It makes me so angry when she's like this. Especially as *she's* the special one. 'How did you know?' I ask her.

'It was such an *obvious* idea,' she says, 'we were bound to think of it too.'

That's what Abby said, but I don't buy it. It's not the recordings. Something else is going on. How do I find out what?

'We just made a few improvements,' she continues.

I want to argue with her, but theirs *is* better. We chose Room 14 because it's our form room. But Room 24 is a room people walk through to get from one half of the building to the other, so it has more passing trade. Also, it's bigger.

'Whoa! Avengers trading cards! How much?!' Mo Hussain pushes past me and I stumble forward, tripping over a bag and spilling its contents.

'Rudeness alert!' I shout at him. 'Didn't they teach you manners at the zoo you grew up in?'

Maxie smiles. Not at me falling over, but at me shouting at Mo. It's like she thinks I'm funny. She likes me. I'm her sister. So what's this meanness about?

I bend down to pick up the bag I tripped over. Maxie bends down too, and I realize it's *her* bag. There's an awkward moment when I start putting things back in the bag and stop. I'm helping her. And I don't want to help her.

'Thanks,' she says.

'You're weird,' I say.

She smiles at that too.

Maybe now's the time to ask her about the 1p. 'Max . . . why—?'

Then I see something in her bag. It's not a textbook – it's a colourful exercise book – and I see the letters *lub* and *ndboo* on it.

'Why *what*?' she says.

Oh my God, the Club Handbook! I have to find out how they know everything.

I *have* to know what they're planning next.

I *have* to see inside that handbook.

'Nothing,' I say, standing up.

Stealing is wrong, obviously. But all's fair in love and war, and this *is* a war. And they started it.

I walk away from Maxie, searching through the masses of boys until I find the Mob. They're standing in a corner with Obi while she shouts at her brothers. She's holding Bem by the shirt. 'You were supposed to bring your friends to Room 14!'

'A trading-card forum needs people there,' he says, trying to stand up to his little sister, but looking scared. 'You know, to trade with.'

He has a point.

'Let him go, Obi,' I say to her. 'He's suffered enough.'

Bem looks grateful, and as soon as Obi releases him he scuttles off.

'Mobsters,' I say, beckoning the girls to me, 'I need you guys to run distraction detail.'

'Huh?' says Candy, who has to learn to watch more spy movies.

I shove the boxes of sweets from Room 14 into their arms. 'I need you to distract the Club – particularly Maxie – while I do something.'

'What are you up to?' asks Abby.

'You'll find out,' I tell her. 'Just start selling these sweets.'

'She won't like that,' says Candy.

'That's the plan,' I tell her.

Abby looks nervous. 'I feel like I'm taking a bullet for the Mob,' she says.

'That's exactly what you are doing,' I tell her. 'A huge Maxie-shaped bullet. Now, go. Serve your Mob.'

With a push from me they head off looking like old-fashioned cinema sweet-sellers, the boxes held out in front of them. I hang back, watching as the three Mobsters walk past Maxie's desk.

'Who wants a sweet?' shouts Obi. 'We also have flyers for our nightclub night next week!'

Maxie's head flicks up.

'There's no way you have hired a whole night-club,' says a boy with ginger hair.

'We have,' says Candy. 'See for yourself.'

This is my chance. While they are all inspecting the flyers I drop and start crawling under the desks.

'*Act Your Age*,' he reads. 'Cool!'

It's pretty disgusting down here; boys never clean their shoes.

'Yup,' says Candy. 'It's just £5 to get in.'

I crawl my way over to Maxie and, more importantly, her bag.

'You can't give out those flyers in here,' she says. But – annoyingly – she's sticking to her spot. 'And you can't sell sweets.'

'Why not?' asks Candy.

I'm under the desk next to Maxie's, waiting for the opportunity to strike.

'Because this is *the Club's* fundraising event.'

Maxie is still not moving. Hannah from the Club is standing just next to me.

'Where does it say that?' Obi asks. 'Have you rented the leasehold off the school board?' Obi's using Maxie's own lines against her. 'Is this some ancient right I don't know about? If so, I'd like to see your papers.'

I cover my mouth to stifle my laughter and accidently brush Hannah's leg with my elbow.

Hannah reaches down and scratches the spot where I touched her.

I have to go. Now. I edge forward towards Maxie's desk.

'Don't be ridiculous.' Maxie's angry. She comes round the desk towards Obi.

I wait until she's passed and dive forward to her bag. I have to do this as quickly as I can, but it's zipped shut. My fingers fumble before I get it open. And then, in among other books and genius home-work papers, it's there: the Club Handbook.

I've got it.

'Who's kicking me?' It's Hannah – my foot brushed her leg again. I scramble forward on hands and knees, then pop up on the other side of the room. I can tell my face is flushed, but when I look round, Maxie is still yelling at Obi, Abby and Candy, and Hannah is looking under the desk to see what touched her.

But I'm here. With the Club Handbook in my arms. And I can't wait to see what's inside.

Chapter 16

'I'm so nervous I can't even eat,' I say to the Mob as I shove a Fun Size Mars bar into my mouth.

The Mob have gathered in our headquarters. The girls from the Club are still in Room 24 for the trading-card thing so there's no chance of them coming in. We've pulled the sheet across, checked the room for recording devices and *still* we're whispering. Can't be too careful.

'Ready?' I ask the others.

'Ready,' they reply in unison.

This feels so sneaky – we are actually spying on the Club, searching through their handbook to see what information we can gather. It doesn't look as cool as our handbook because it wasn't designed by Abby. Their logo is just a club symbol from a deck of cards, which I suppose is quite clever, but totally ugly compared to our star logo.

'Plain black,' says Abby. 'No thought gone into the design at all.'

We open it to the first page. What instantly annoys me is that it's set out exactly like our Mob Handbook. Ours is a file, so it's easier to split into sections – they've had to stick tabs to the pages of theirs. It means ours is better . . . but still. The first page is a title page. The second is a register. The third lists the money they've raised – with a felt-pen thermometer. The fourth has some ideas they've had for charity events.

'Let's see what they've come up with,' says Obi.

They've listed a jumble sale, a raffle, a movie shown at lunchtime. They've got everything we came up with on the first day and then dismissed because it was too boring. They've crossed a few things out and written notes around other things.

'They've got nothing! The Club wouldn't know a good idea if they were following it on Twitter,' I say, unable to keep the glee out of my voice.

'Car wash?!' says Obi. 'How could the school do a car wash?'

We're feeling pretty pleased with ourselves, looking around and congratulating each other for being – easily – the best club. I pass round the sweets and we all take some. Even Abby takes a handful of Gummy Bears. I'm glad to see she's feeling better too.

We flick through more pages of their handbook, more registers, more bad ideas. 'They've gone off topic here,' says Obi as we hit a page that lists *Hillcrest Super Crushes*.

'Ooooh, let me see,' says Candy. She grabs the book and starts reading. 'OMG, did you know that Sonia Palmer fancies Kyle Rosen?'

I pull a puke face. Kyle Rosen has really hairy eyebrows. We all laugh.

'Does Donna really fancy Reece?'

Candy bites her lip as she looks up at me. Then she nods slowly. 'Sorry, Tara,' she says.

I grab the book off her. There it is in black and white, underlined in purple pen and surrounded by a red heart.

Donna: Reece Lee.

I want to write something rude next to it, but I need to get the handbook back into Maxie's bag before she notices it's gone. I check my watch. We have to be back in our form rooms at one fifteen. This means we have just ten minutes to get as much information as we can.

I flip through more random pages, more doodles – *wait!*

'What is it?' asks Candy, who has obviously seen my expression change.

I flip back a page to see a register that looks different to the others.

The Club has five members: Maxie, Donna, Sonia, Hannah and Indiana. But suddenly, on this page, today at break time, there is an extra person on the list.

Someone named 'the Mole'.

I don't show the others yet. I look at each register in turn.

'What?' says Abby. 'If you've seen anything that affects the Mob, then you must tell.'

I *must* tell. They have an extra member. A member so secret that she's been given a code name. It could be Simone – the girl in our year that keeps herself to herself – but I haven't seen her speak to anyone. And 'the Mole' is hardly the most subtle of code names.

'We've got a spy,' I say.

'What?' they all say together.

'One of you is a spy.'

Candy covers her mouth with her hand. Obi clenches her fists. Abby stops chewing her sweets.

'What dwo ywow mean?' she says, mouth full.

'Look.' I turn the book round to show them. 'A meeting with the Mole'.

'What's a mole?' asks Candy.

Is she dumb, or is she just *playing* dumb?

'A mole is a spy. Someone who enters an organization, but really they are a double agent – working for the other side.' I look at her hard when I say this. Then Obi. Then Abby.

'You'd better not be thinking it's me,' says Obi. 'I have no reason to betray the Mob.'

'Neither do *any* of us!' says Abby.

'Well, it's not me,' Candy stutters. 'D-d-d-definitely not me.'

'Why is your face red?' I say. 'Why do you look so guilty?'

'It's like I said the other day,' Candy says, crossing her arms in front of her chest, then changing her mind and dropping them to her side.

'Sometimes people look guilty without having done anything wrong.'

'*Pffft!*' Obi spits.

Candy goes even redder. 'It's not me!'

But suddenly it all makes sense. 'What about Donna?' Candy has always seemed kind of afraid, kind of obsessed with Donna. 'You'd do anything to get in with her . . . You approached the Mob only *after* Donna wouldn't let you in her 3Ms.'

Candy's mouth drops open. 'Well . . .' She's thinking of a defence. Classic sign of guilt. 'What about your sister?'

I'm lost for words for a moment. Abby gasps. Accusing others is another classic sign of guilt.

'Do you think I'd spy on my own club?' I say.

'If you think *we* could be spies,' says Candy, 'there's no reason we shouldn't think *you're* the spy.'

I start stammering too now, mainly because I *know* I am not the spy. 'D-don't be ridiculous!'

'Now that I think about it,' says Candy, 'Maxie and Tara must be working together. It isn't plausible that Maxie would be so cool and Tara . . . you know . . . not.'

Ouch! 'What do you mean?' I can't believe she's being so rude. She must be hitting out because we're on to her. 'Are you saying that Maxie's Club is better than the Mob?'

'No . . . it's just . . .'

I've caught her out now. 'Is that why you've been spying for them. Because you're secretly one of them?'

'No!' she shouts. 'I'm just saying that you might—'

'Sorry to have to do this,' I say, 'but all the evidence points to Candy. I vote that we expel her from the Mob.'

'What evidence?' she yelps.

'You have opportunity, living next door to Donna,' says Abby. 'And motive too: you wanted to be in her club from the very beginning.'

'The colour of your face says it all,' adds Obi. 'No one goes that shade of red unless they have something to hide.'

There are tears in Candy's eyes. I start feeling bad, start feeling uncertain. But she is the most likely suspect – other than me.

Abby puts up her hand. 'I second the motion to expel Candy.'

I put up my hand too. I was the one who made the motion in the first place, so I guess I have to.

A tear falls from Candy's eye and it makes me feel rubbish.

Obi looks from us to Candy, then slowly puts her hand up. 'Sorry, Candy.'

I feel a little sick as I remove the scoobie Candy made from my wrist. I'm not turning into a bitch like Donna, am I? Abby and Obi quickly do the same, handing their scoobies to me. I give all three to Candy.

'Take these.' I sound firm, but inside I'm a wobbly mess.

Candy starts gulping as she gets up, pushes the sheet aside and stumbles out of the meeting room. 'But I didn't do anything,' she sobs as she goes.

That can't be true, I tell myself. Nobody hasn't done *anything*. We're all guilty of *something*. But Candy's tears seem real. And as the door to the toilets slams shut I wonder if we've just made a big mistake . . .

Chapter 17

'You two order whatever you like,' says Dad.

It's Friday night. We're spending the weekend at Dad's, and he's taking us out for pizza.

'What about you?' I ask.

'I'm not hungry,' he says, which is a bit weird, but I'm used to my family being weird by now.

I've hardly said a word to Maxie since . . . basically since she became a big fat betrayer. We have separate rooms at Mum's, so it's easy to ignore her. But at Dad's we have to share. She's sitting opposite me with a blank expression on her face. I can't tell if she's sad, or embarrassed, or proud of herself.

'Not hungry, Dad?' she asks, sounding like she's accusing him of secretly liking country music. Which annoys me. It's like she's angry with him, when it should be the other way round. Yeah, things have changed over the last two weeks, but it's her fault for getting chucked out of her old school. And with both me and Maxie living at Mum's now, Dad's all by himself.

'That's what I said,' he says.

There's this gigantic silence in the air and I guess that Maxie and Dad have issues that are bigger than I ever guessed. It's weird to think that while she was going to WSG and living with Dad they had a life of their own that Mum and I knew nothing about.

'Well, I'm starving!' I say, trying to lighten the mood. 'I could eat two whole pizzas and still have room for dessert.'

Dad ruffles my hair. 'Two pizzas? Really?'

'We could share a pizza,' says Maxie. 'I don't mind sharing with Tara if you can't afford it.'

Dad frowns at Maxie.

I didn't think of that. Because he works freelance, Dad doesn't have as much money as Mum and he has to think about things that Mum never really has to worry about.

'I was only joking about the two pizzas,' I say.

'It's fine, Dad,' says Maxie. 'I'm sure Tara won't mind sharing.'

'No, no.' He doesn't sound completely happy. 'I said you could have what you like, and I meant it.'

There is another awkward silence. About the nine hundredth since Dad picked us up. Finally he sighs and gets up from the table. 'I'll be back in a sec,' he says.

While he's in the loo I'm stuck with Maxie and it's impossible to ignore her.

'Come on, let's share,' I say, forcing some enthusiasm into my voice.

'OK,' she says. 'You can choose what we have.'

'What?' I say. 'Anything?'

'Anything,' she says with a nod.

I do my super-villain smile. 'Even pineapple?' I ask, knowing that Maxie hates to mix sweet and savoury.

'Even' – she does an over-the-top gulp – 'pineapple.'

'What about pineapple and tuna?' I say, wiggling my eyebrows.

'That sounds . . .' She gulps again, but she's trying not to laugh. 'Some people might think pineapple and tuna is a gross combination, but I think it sounds innovative. Not many pizzas contain one of your five-a-day.'

'Ha!' I say. 'How true. Then I think we should go for mushrooms too.' Maxie thinks mushrooms were sent from another planet to kill her.

'So, you want tuna, mushroom and pineapple?' she says. 'Tara Simmons, I think you might have invented the most disgusting pizza topping in the entire world! I'm proud of you.'

A waitress comes over. 'Are you girls ready to order?'

'We'd like to share a large tuna, mushroom and pineapple pizza,' Maxie says. She makes a gagging noise, then points at me.

'Really?' asks the waitress. 'Are you trying to win a bet?'

'No,' I tell her. 'She's joking. We'd like a large pepperoni.'

Even though I prefer quattro formaggi, I know Maxie is all about the meat. Weirdly, we seem to be getting along. Why spoil it for the sake of four different kinds of cheese?

'With extra pepperoni,' I say. 'And two Cokes, please.'

The waitress writes on her pad and gathers up our menus. 'Hey,' she says. I know what she's about to ask. Everyone asks the same thing. 'Are you twins?'

'No. We're just sisters of the same age.' We both automatically say this. We've been saying it for years.

The waitress looks confused – the usual response to our answer. 'You're cute,' she says. 'It must be nice to have such a close relationship. My sister annoys the hell out of me.' She looks really sad. And then she walks away.

There is another silence, but this one isn't really awkward, more thoughtful.

'Max . . .' I start. I'm nervous, but I have to ask. 'Why did you do it?'

Maxie's smile drops and she looks at her lap.

'You stole 1p,' I remind her. 'That's, like, really strange.'

Maxie's stare doesn't leave her lap.

'Mum and Dad will make you have counselling. They'll think you've gone crazy. They won't give up until you tell them.' I take a deep breath and ask, 'Did you mean to steal more?'

Maxie shakes her head. 'If I'd wanted to steal more, I could have.'

It's like I've insulted her intelligence.

'Then . . . why?'

Maxie sighs. 'I did it because I wanted to prove I could.'

'Prove it to *who*? The bank's lax security systems? A criminal gang?' I'm trying to make this conversation easy, but she's not making it easy on me.

'I wanted to show Mum and Dad I knew . . .'

'Knew *what*?' That's the weirdest explanation of them all.

'Look, Tara, you're Mum and Dad's favourite.' She says it like it shouldn't come as a shock to me – like the sun is round, or poo smells. 'You came along eleven months after me and stole all my baby-cooing thunder. Mum likes you better than she likes me. But *Dad*? Well, I might as well not exist when it comes to him.'

'Don't be ridiculous,' I say.

'If we were both in a burning building, he would rescue you first . . . And if he had time to rescue me too, he might not even bother.' Maxie looks at the seat Dad left.

'Oh whatever, Maxie! Stop acting crazy. He loves you. And he's being great today,' I say, 'really treating us.'

Maxie rolls her eyes. 'Yeah, it's nice of *Mum* to treat us.'

'What are you talking about?' Her know-it-all attitude is really annoying. 'What has this got to do with Mum?'

Maxie doesn't answer. Instead she fiddles with her paper place mat.

It must be weird for Maxie that I used to spend more time with Mum than she did. But it's weird for me that she spent more time with Dad. I miss him; he misses me. Just like Mum missed Max when she wasn't there. Mum was always low after Maxie went back to Dad's every week. Maxie didn't see it, but I did. She'd take a glass of wine into her room and shut the door.

'So what if Dad spoils us a little when I'm around?' I say to her. 'Mum spoils you. She took you on that shopping spree on my birthday – got you a haircut and new clothes – and I never said anything.'

Maxie sighs. 'Tara, you are so naive,' she says to the place mat. 'It's only Mum that treats us.'

I nearly forget what the waitress said about sisters and think about punching Maxie for being so patronizing.

'Dad doesn't have any money,' she says.

Slowly things drop into place and I see where she's going with this.

'Most divorces, the man pays the woman maintenance. But Mum has to give Dad money every month.'

This is brand-new information. It does my head in a little.

'Even now she has both of us almost all the time, she *still* gives him money.'

I feel really stupid for not thinking about this before. Of course Mum gives Dad money; she earns loads and Dad earns almost nothing.

'Oh.'

'Yeah,' says Maxie.

Sometimes it's really obvious that Maxie is a genius and I am just her thicko baby sister.

'And you know how rubbish Dad is with that stuff . . .' Maxie goes on.

I do know. When Mum and Dad were together and he was a stay-at-home dad, one week he'd be cooking fillet steaks every night. Then there would be a huge argument and it was leftovers, tinned food and spaghetti bolognese for days.

'When I was living with Dad it took me a while to work out why sometimes we lived like millionaires – movies, ice cream, new clothes – but the second half of the month we were like Victorian paupers. Sometimes he didn't eat dinner and only made food for me. Beans on toast or whatever.'

'I like beans on toast,' I say.

Maxie pretends not to hear me. 'So I took a guess, and checked out to see if I was right. I hacked into his computer and saw his bank account. Money from Mum went in every month.'

'You hacked into Dad's bank account?'

Mum and Dad raised us to respect people's privacy. We were told never to read people's diaries, letters, or anything like that. Then suddenly the image of the Club Handbook I took flashes across my mind and I remember that snooping is easier to justify than I thought.

'I know that was bad,' she replies, 'but I didn't take any money or anything. I was just looking.'

'You didn't take any money *that* time,' I remind her.

I think about the idea that Mum gives Dad money. It's a bit of a shock, but then I think, *So what?* What's the difference between Mum giving Dad money and Dad giving Mum money?

'So what if Mum is richer than Dad?' I say to Maxie. 'So what if she pays him maintenance? That's equal rights, and what happens when people get divorced. Just because you had to eat a few portions of beans on toast from time to time, your life is still a lot better than a lot of people's!'

'I don't have a life better than yours,' she says softly, closing her eyes for a little too long.

This is the final straw. I push my chair back and stand up. 'I'm going to find Dad and see if he's OK.' This must be why Dad's not eating; he's splurging on us and starving himself. 'Enjoy your pizza. It's all yours, you greedy pig!'

I push my chair back and head for the toilets. He's been a long time. I shove the door to the men's loos and shout, 'Dad!' before it swings back shut again.

No reply.

But if he's not in the toilet, where is he?

Just next to the restaurant is a pub. He wouldn't leave us and go there, would he? But I can't think where else he could be. I know I'm not allowed to go in alone, but this is an emergency: I need to tell Dad I love him.

And there he is, standing by a fruit machine. He looks miserable. Miserable enough to leave his daughters at a restaurant while he gets some peace. He feeds coins into the slot.

'Dad!' I call.

He turns, and when he sees it's me looks very worried. 'Are you OK, Tata?' he says, calling me by my baby name. 'Sorry I left just now, but—'

I run to him and his expression changes. He opens his arms.

'What's up, sweetie?' he says as he hugs me.

'Nothing.' I sniffle into his chest. 'I just love you.'

'Aw, little Tata.' He hugs me tighter. 'I love you too. Come on, let's go and finish that pizza.' He throws a last look back to the fruit machine and we head out of the pub, hand in hand.

Chapter 18

As the bell goes for the end of the first class on Monday morning Candy runs out of the classroom. All five members of the Club are waiting for her outside and they welcome her with open arms – literally – hugging when she joins them. Their Candy-made scoobies dangle from their wrists.

'Mole,' Obi sneers.

Candy throws her a look.

I'd like to say that it's made me feel better that we didn't falsely accuse Candy, but it doesn't. She's a traitor, and it hurts like hell. Also, I feel stupid that we thought our club's business was secret, when she probably told them everything ages ago. Our ideas to raise money. Our secret knock. Our handshake.

Obi and Abby come and stand next to me and we push our way past the Club. 'I'm calling a Mob meeting,' I say. 'There's something important I want to discuss.'

We walk out arm in arm, with me in the middle. It's Craig Hurst who points out the obvious. 'Your club seems to have shrunk,' he says. Then he looks over at Maxie and her lot. 'Six against three,' he says. 'Not looking good for you, is it?'

'So you've finally learned to count?' I say. 'Well done you.'

'It's quality, not quantity, Craig,' says Obi. 'How much money have *you* raised?'

'I absolutely guarantee I'll get more money than you,' he says. He looks really pleased with himself. 'It'll be me and my mates' – he looks at Phil, Mo and Matt – 'going to Alton Towers, not you.'

I forgot that's why we are doing all of this. It's always seemed like we were doing it just so we could beat the Club, and beat my stupid genius sister. It kind of slipped my mind that we were raising money to buy Becky a wheelchair and win a prize.

'Let the best girl win,' I say to him.

'Duhhh,' Phil says, rolling his eyes. 'He's not a girl.'

'Oh,' I say, 'my mistake.' Obi and I start giggling as we head to the loos.

But Abby looks worried. 'You shouldn't have a go at him like that,' she says.

'Oh, what's he going to do?' I reply.

Abby frowns.

Once we get into the girls' loos, we go to Mob HQ and hang the sheet up.

'I call here present the first inaugural meeting of the three-member Mob,' I say, to sound official.

'I think inaugural *means* first,' says Obi.

I shake my head. 'What's with the IQ explosion?'

They laugh. But none of us is completely happy.

'So why are we here?' asks Abby. 'Got another money-raising scheme?'

'Did you see that the Club are up to £288 now?' says Obi.

I did see. We thought we did really well over the weekend, getting over the £250 mark. Abby has given up colouring the thermometer in. I guess it seems a little pathetic now. But we still have the nightclub event . . . all our hopes of winning are pinned on that one night.

But that's not what I want to talk about.

'We are at war. There is no denying it now,' I say. 'They spied on us, we tricked them. We stole their handbook, and now they are bound to retaliate.' I realize that I'm talking like Winston Churchill, but the other two are going with it, so I continue. 'Firstly,' I say, pulling out a padlock and three keys from my bag, 'we are going to keep our handbook under lock and key. Up there, locked in the vent.'

I give each of the girls a key to the padlock.

'Look, ladies,' I say, 'I trust you both. I really do. And by giving us all equal access to the handbook, I hope it shows you can trust me.'

Both of them nod quickly.

'But the Mob had a mole before, and it could happen again.'

Both of them shake their heads. 'No way,' says Abby.

'The sanctity of the Mob is too important to risk.'

Obi giggles. She loves it when I do the solemn speech thing.

I take a step back in the room. It looks huge now, with only three of us in here. It just emphasizes what we've lost.

'So I have an idea: a test of loyalty.'

Abby squeezes her eyes shut. 'Is it going to hurt?' she asks.

I laugh, despite the solemn stuff I was just doing. 'Nothing like that! No, this is more serious than pain.' I pause for dramatic effect. 'We each have to give up our biggest secret.'

Suddenly neither Obi nor Abby can look me in the eye. Seems they both have secrets. Just like me.

'But . . .' says Obi.

'We'll write down our secrets, file them in the handbook, then lock the handbook in the vent,' I say.

Abby shakes her head. 'I'm not sure . . .'

Obi's shaking her head too.

'They'll be in code, so we can't easily read them.'

There's a pause in the head-shaking.

'We will promise to *never* read each other's secrets,' I say.

'So why . . . ?' Obi starts to ask, but then she gets it.

'Not unless that person is revealed to be a traitor,' I finish.

Abby looks up. 'So it's like insurance?'

'Yes,' I say. 'The Mob keeps hold of the secrets. Only we know how to decode them. But the Mob won't read them unless that person betrays us.'

'And we've all given up a secret so we all have the same amount to lose,' adds Obi. 'Makes sense.'

I nod.

Obi nods.

Abby hesitates, then nods.

This is a good idea. We all do the Mob handshake, circling our palms and then shaking hands.

I rip a piece of paper out of my pad then I motion for them all to turn around so we have our backs to each other.

'The letter *A* doesn't have to be four places forward,' I tell them. 'Put it wherever you want in the alphabet, so it's more difficult to decode.'

I write out the alphabet at the top and then write it again, this time with the *A* seven places forward.

I write my secret. Fold over the top so Abby and Obi can't see, then pass the paper over my head to Obi. She does the same, passing it to Abby.

'You all done?' I ask, when Abby's finished.

'Yup,' they say.

I put the folded piece of paper into the Mob Handbook. Then the other two give me a leg-up and I put the handbook in the vent. Then I lock the vent with the padlock.

'And let no man tear asunder . . .' says Obi, doing the solemn speak, but her voice is shaking a little.

'Now we can all be brilliant, trustworthy, faithful friends,' I say, trying to sound chirpy. But as soon as the words are out of my mouth I realize that what we've done is the exact opposite of faith . . . we have a hold over each other.

From the beginning, the point of the Mob was raising money and making friends. But this doesn't feel like friendship. It feels horrible.

Chapter 19

For the past five minutes I've been subtly putting my pens in my pencil case while Mrs Saleem drones on about medieval crop rotation. It's 3.12 p.m. I want to be the first one out of here. Normally I don't like history, but it's a class where neither Abby nor Obi is with me, and at least it means I can get out and get home without having to speak to them. I would feel bad, but I think they're doing the same thing.

We've been spending a bit of time together to raise money and stuff, but it's as if all the fun has been taken out of it. There's been this icky feeling between us ever since we made the Secret Insurance. I'm hoping it will pass . . . We made a plan to get ready together at my house before the nightclub night tomorrow. I'm sure a girlie night of doing hair and make-up will fix everything.

The bell goes. Everyone scrapes their chairs back in a hurry.

'Class! Homework . . .' Mrs Saleem calls out, but no one seems to be listening. 'Read chapter 5 for next week.'

I don't bother to write it in my homework diary.

Someone taps me on the shoulder. It's Sean Flynn, a boy I sit next to in geography.

'Hey, Tara,' he says.

'Hi,' I say, but don't stop throwing my things into my bag.

'I heard about this awesome nightclub party you're having tomorrow,' he says.

This is so cool! If Sean Flynn knows about the fundraiser, hopefully everyone is talking about it. We're going to raise a heap of money and beat the Club.

'Is it for real? You've actually got a nightclub?'

'I wouldn't say it if it wasn't true.'

'And can anyone come?'

'Of course!' I say. 'It's a fundraiser – we want as many people there as possible.'

Sean looks pleased. He shrugs his coat on and is about to leave when he turns back and says, 'You know Reece Lee, don't you?'

He knows me and Reece are friends? Does that mean Reece talks about me? 'Yup,' I say. 'I've known him for years. Since my old school.' I can't hide the smile on my face.

'Cool,' he says. 'Do you know if he's with that fit girl?'

My beam drops. 'Which fit girl?' There are only ten girls in the whole school, but the idea that there's only one 'fit girl' is gutting. Especially as it's not me. And worse, I think I know who he's talking about.

'The brown-haired girl . . . with the hair.'

Donna.

It hits me hard.

'No,' I say. 'He's definitely not *with* her.'

Sean slings his backpack over one shoulder. 'But he's always doing band practice with her these days. If he's not her boyfriend, he definitely wants to be.'

I can't give him up without a fight. I've liked Reece for too long.

Guessing that they'll be in one of the music rooms, I head over there and walk down past the row of doors. I hear a cello in one room, someone doing piano scales in the next, a very squeaky violin, then I hear what sounds like a CD. A proper band with the full arrangement of drums, guitar and everything. They sound amazing! Then comes the singing:

'♫ *Crying's not enough to make you mine . . .* ♫'

Oh wow, that's Donna. And annoyingly, she's good.

'♫ *Begging's not gonna work this time . . .* ♫'

Sucker Punch is awesome. I might have to get the album, even if the lead singer *is* Donna Woods.

I knock on the door, but of course they can't hear, so I nudge it open.

Reece is on the drums, his hair flying up every time he whacks his sticks down. It's Joel who's the first to notice me. He stops. Then Lenny stops. Then Reece stops and looks up from his drums – wondering why they've messed up the song, I guess. Then he sees me and he looks somewhere between happy and confused as to why I would barge in.

'♫ *I'll wait forever just to make you see-ee-ee . . .* ♫'

Apparently nothing will stop this girl. She's got one finger in her ear and her eyes squeezed tight shut. She turns to face Reece.

'♫ *No one will love you like me-ee-ee . . .* ♫'

And she does this last part really slowly. Without seeing her face I can't tell for sure, but the shocked look from Reece means she's probably gazing right into his eyes as she sings a cappella.

'That sounds great with no accompaniment on the last line,' she says. 'Just me. Good call.'

Reece winces at her, then nods in my direction. Donna turns, and has the exact opposite reaction to Reece – she scowls. And blushes.

'What do you want?' she asks.

'You know what, Donna . . .' I start.

'What?' she says, putting a hand on her hip.

'You guys sound great.'

Her mouth makes a perfect *O*. She drops her hand. That's thrown her. 'Umm . . . thanks.'

'Anyway . . . I just wanted to ask Reece something.' As soon as I say that so blatantly, *I* start to blush. 'Er . . . I mean, I wanted to ask *all of you* something!' I backpedal, but it's too late. Lenny and Joel smirk at each other over their guitars.

'What are you doing tomorrow?' I ask. 'Because, I don't know if you heard' – I wave the flyers Abby made – 'but we're having a fundraiser thing at Boulevard nightclub.'

'*Heard?*' says Lenny. 'It's all anyone can talk about!'

'It's *not* all anyone can talk about,' says Donna. 'The Club have organized a raffle. Now *that's* exciting!' She waves her arms, jazz-hands style.

The boys go silent. I catch Reece's eye and we both have to look at the floor to stop ourselves laughing.

'So you're definitely coming then?' I ask Reece, and then shift my position so it looks as if I'm asking all of them.

'Ummm . . .' Joel looks worried. 'Do you know if – um – Abby will be there?' He rubs the back of his head as he asks.

OMG! Joel likes Abby. I was right! Maybe now she'll finally believe me when I tell her she's gorgeous.

'Of course she will!' I say. 'She designed the flyer.' Joel's face lights up. 'She's in the Mob. One of the founding members and—'

Donna splutters.

'What?' I say.

'Nothing,' she says.

I ignore Donna. I've just had two pieces of brilliant news in the space of two seconds: everyone at Hillcrest is excited about the fundraiser. Everyone except the Club – which kind of makes it even better. And Joel fancies Abby.

'Has anyone *seen* Abby, by the way?' I ask. 'She hasn't been around much all week.'

'Have you tried the pool?' asks Lenny. 'She's usually there at lunch, and after school. Sometimes before school.'

Is she?

'She's probably bunked off,' Donna says, examining her nails.

Abby doesn't bunk off. We once talked about bunking a maths test, but we were too scared. Donna is up to something, but I'm not going to give her the satisfaction of asking what.

'She'll be at the shops. Buying clothes,' Donna continues. 'Spending all her money.'

'What are you on about?'

Dammit! I asked. And the satisfaction is written all over Donna's face.

'I think you'll find that Abby has *looooads* of money at the moment.'

I roll my eyes at her smirk.

'And she'll be spending it all on clothes. You know, seeing as she's lost so much weight.'

Huh?

'Haven't you noticed?' she asks.

'Has she?' I can't help but ask. I'm supposed to be her best friend and I've been completely oblivious.

Donna grabs up her bag from the side of the room. 'We were all saying she should write one of those diet columns: the Not-So-Flabby-Any-More-Abby Diet.' She walks towards me with her phone. 'Check this out.'

She pulls up the photo from our Introduction Day at Hillcrest – the one Mrs Martin took of all the boys' school girls together. Abby is there, of course, and Donna's right . . . she looks different. Way heavier. How did she lose all that in just three weeks? How did I not notice? I guess when you see the same person every day, you don't pick up on the gradual changes. Still, I feel pretty bad. Now all the refusals of takeaways and sweets make more sense.

But more to the point – how is this healthy? It's way too much weight to lose in such a short time.

I swipe through Donna's photos. 'Have you got any more of Abby?' What she does have is loads of pictures of herself in various outfits.

'No!' she says, clearly realizing what I'm looking at. She reaches out to grab the phone, but I whisk it away from her.

'Very nice!' In this one she's wearing leg-warmers and a ripped T-shirt. From the fluorescent headband I guess she was going for an eighties look.

She grabs for her phone again, and I don't want to be too mean so I hand it back to her.

'Love that pout,' I say with a wink.

But then Lenny snatches the phone. 'I wanna see,' he says. He's just teasing her, and the other two join in.

Lenny holds it above his head and Donna jumps for it. She's smiling. She's loving the attention. Particularly when Reece comes round from behind his drums and grabs her by the wrists.

This makes my heart lurch a bit. I try to tell myself it's band bonding, but I hate him holding her like that. And I *really* hate how she's not even trying to get away.

'Good look!' says Joel. 'Is that your mum's wedding dress?'

He turns the phone round to show us, and it's Donna in a lilac dress with a gigantic skirt. And she has a tea towel veil on her head.

'Nooooo,' she says, but she's laughing. 'I was trying it on for a dare.'

'I don't see anyone daring you,' Lenny says.

Donna laughs, and we all join in.

Lenny swipes through a few more. 'That's it,' he says. 'Shame. That cheered me right up.'

He hands the phone to me to hand back to Donna. I'm about to pass it across when I see something on the screen I half recognize. It's a photo of a piece of paper. A piece of paper with writing on it: a load of nonsense words written out in capitals.

Oh God. It's code.

Donna gasps. She knows as well as I do what I am looking at. 'Give it back,' she says.

But I don't. At the top of the page is my writing. There are two more sentences below it – Obi's and Abby's secrets.

'Give me back my phone, Tara.'

Donna has my secret. My coded secret. The one that was supposed to be locked away in the vent.

It might look like:

P YLDYVAL TF ZPZALY'Z WLYZVUHS ZAHALTLUA AV NLA OLY PUAV DVRPUNOHT ZJOVVS MVY AOL NPMALK

But I know it says:

I rewrote my sister's personal statement to get her into Wokingham School for the Gifted.

'Where did you get this?' I'm not shouting, but the boys stop moving because they can tell whatever it is is a big deal.

There is still a mole in the Mob. Or maybe Candy *was* the Mole, but the Club have recruited another.

'Er . . .' Donna takes a deep breath.

For one paranoid moment I wonder if *everyone* is a mole and the Mob is just a way for Maxie to make me look stupid.

Maxie. Oh God. What if she reads it?

'You didn't show these to anyone, did you?' I ask Donna.

Donna wiggles her head and says, 'I might have. I might not,' with a huge grin on her face.

'Donna, this is serious!' I shout. 'Has Maxine seen this photo?'

Donna takes a step away from me.

'Please, Donna! Please say you didn't show this to Maxie.'

Donna drops the grin. 'I WhatsApped it over to her about ten minutes ago.' She's gone a bit pale now too.

This is bad. I'm already backing out the door.

'But what's the big deal, Tara?' asks Reece. 'It's gibberish. No one could work out what it says.'

No one except my sister, the genius.

Chapter 20

My heart's beating heavily in my chest, partly because I have been running my absolute fastest, partly because I am so scared.

You know that thing in nightmares where you do something awful? So awful it can't be taken back? Well, this feels like that, only I'm just not waking up.

I rewrote my sister's personal statement so she could get into the school she wanted. Apparently my essay was the best they'd ever had. But that thought doesn't make me smile any more.

I'm shaking as I put my key into the front door at Mum's house. As soon as I open it I see Maxie's school bag dumped on the floor.

'Maxie!' I shout. Running up the stairs two at a time. 'Maxie, stop! Don't read it!'

I'm just hoping, if this can't be a nightmare, that there is a chance she hasn't worked it out yet.

But when I think back to how quickly she deciphered our code last time, I know the odds of that are very, very small.

I slam into her bedroom door. It won't open.

'Max, open up.'

No answer. I push again, but she must have something wedged against the door because it's budging just a bit.

'Maxie, I'm coming in whether you like it or not.'

'Go away.' It's a relief to hear her voice. But not a huge one.

'Let me explain,' I say. I give the door one almighty shove and it opens just enough for me to squeeze through. The back of her armchair was against it and I have to climb over it to get in.

Maxie is sitting on the floor in the middle of the room, her head bent, her hair covering her eyes. She has her phone – I can make out the image on the screen from here – the Mob secrets. And she has lots of paper around her. I am happy to see it's taken her a few goes to get it . . . but she has got it. Or at least, she has enough of it.

I REWROTE MY SISTER'S PERSONAL STATEMENT TO GET HER INTO WOKIN

There it is. In black and white – written in my sister's block capitals.

'Is this true?' she whispers.

Her face is so wet from crying that some of her hair is plastered to her cheek.

'Umm . . .' Where do I start? 'Yes,' I say.

That hangs in the air for a minute. It isn't very often that Maxie looks confused, so her frowning, concentrating face is a new one on me.

'Sorry, Maxie, but . . .' I want to explain myself. I wish this had come out at any other time. We used to be friends. We used to hang out loads at the shopping centre, on Gorgeous Guy Safari. And if we still were friends she'd know I did it because I love her.

'I was trying to help,' I say. I sit on the floor opposite her.

'*Help?*'

'Yes.' I know I did the wrong thing, but I'm feeling defensive as it must be so obvious that I did it for the right reasons. 'I was helping you get into WSG. I thought you *wanted* to go to WSG!'

I remember how it was a year and a half ago when one of the teachers at Rimewood suggested Maxie might be clever enough to go to a special school. Before that, we all knew she was smart – she'd been put in the year ahead of herself, and she'd got *A*s and distinctions since she was sticking bits of pasta on to paper. But we never guessed she was gifted – like proper, genius smart.

Maxie was chuffed. Mum and Dad were chuffed. So chuffed that they were even being nice to each other.

'I thought it would make everyone happy if you got in.'

I'm too embarrassed to admit that I thought it might even stop Mum and Dad from divorcing. The papers were with the lawyers at the time, but no one had signed anything. I hoped they'd want to stay together to support their child prodigy.

'I did it for you.'

But the opposite happened: Dad's rented flat was so close to WSG that it worked even better for them to live apart.

'For me?' shouts Maxie, her eyes flashing. 'You've humiliated me!'

I lean forward to take her hand, but she pulls away. 'I don't get it . . .' I say. And I really don't.

'Let me paint a picture for you,' she says. 'I'm great at maths, we all know this. But you might be surprised to know that I was not the best mathematician at the school. I was, like, slightly better than average – they put me in the second set.'

That does surprise me.

'When I arrived at WSG they were expecting someone who was good at English too. They called me an *all-rounder*. Said I was an anomaly for being excellent at maths *and* English. They put me in the top set.' Maxie smiles as she remembers; she looks proud of herself. Then the smile drops, and I know what's coming next. 'But I was rubbish, really rubbish. Turns out I can't analyse a poem to save my life.'

I read poetry for fun.

'They kept me in set one for about six weeks before realizing their mistake. They moved me down a set, then another, until finally I hit the bottom.'

So Maxie dropping all those sets *was* my fault.

'Do you think no one in the genius school noticed?' She jumps up from the floor and starts pacing. 'The nicer ones asked me what had happened, why my English skills were so much worse than the teachers expected. The meaner ones laughed at me.'

'I'm so sorry, Maxie,' I say.

'I knew I was rubbish at English, but somehow I thought it was a mistake – like maybe the teachers at Rimewood didn't get my writing because it was too far above them. The worst thing was, *I* got my hopes up.'

I feel a bit dizzy from watching her pace. Or maybe it's the guilt. 'Isn't it enough to be brilliant at maths?' I ask.

She rounds on me. 'You'd think,' she says. 'But in a school where everyone is defined by how clever they are – the stupider people get teased by everyone else. I never really had any friends.'

I always thought Maxie didn't have any friends because she was shy. It turns out that was my fault too.

'It might have been OK if they'd known I was no good at English from the start – but to go from all-rounder to no-hoper was really uncool.'

I dropped down a set in chemistry last year. People laughed at me. I can't believe I've let that happen to Maxie too.

'Then I would come home,' she says, pacing again. 'To Dad's place. You and Mum weren't there. We never had any money or any food in the house. There was a £30 school trip to Oxford University, but Dad didn't have the money to pay for me to go.'

I remember Mrs Eames bringing that up. 'Is that why you shouted at that teacher?' I ask.

'Mrs Critcher kept asking me why I didn't want to go, saying that Oxford would be a perfect university for me. But it wasn't that I didn't want to go . . . I couldn't.' Her lip starts wobbling.

That sounds pretty bad. 'Why didn't you ask Mum for the money?'

'Dad told me not to,' she says.

I can't believe he would do that. He wouldn't make his daughter suffer just to cover his tracks. Not my dad. No way.

'One time Dad even pawned the TV to raise some cash. I had no TV for a whole week!'

Is she lying? She doesn't look like she's lying. 'You always had a TV whenever I came round,' I say.

'He somehow got it back. For you. He made me promise not say anything about that either.'

Dad must have been ashamed of having no money. And poor Maxie had to keep the secret too. Now I understand why she's angry with him all the time.

This is the secret life that Maxie had with Dad.

'You and Mum would tell me about the movies you'd been watching together, the takeaways you were eating, the shopping sprees you'd been on. All your millions of friends would come round and you'd be having a great time hanging out with my mum, without a care in the world . . .' She stops pacing and turns to me, but her eyes are closed. 'And without me.'

I can't believe I didn't know any of this.

'You should have said something,' I say. 'You shouldn't have been . . .' I tail off because it would sound pretty big-headed if I've got this wrong.

'You can say it: jealous!' Her eyes snap open and she yells. 'Of *course* I was jealous of you! You're richer than me. You're prettier than me. You're more popular than me. You're funny and fun. You have loads of friends who adore you. You came along so soon after I did that Mum and Dad really struggled.'

I guess I always knew that having two babies in the space of a year was really hard for Mum and Dad. I say out loud what I have been wondering all my life. 'Maybe they would have got on better if I had never been born.'

Maxie throws her hands in the air. 'Are you kidding?' she says. 'You're the light of their lives.'

I have never thought of myself like this.

'The only thing I had, Tara, was the fact that I was clever and you weren't. But now I find out that you're clever too. And it kills me.'

Wow. I had no idea. I guess everyone wants to be special. Genius was Maxie's thing, and I took it from her. Just like she took Hillcrest from me.

She drops her chin to her chest. 'I'm not your twin. I'm just your second-rate, slightly older sister.' She raises her head slowly and looks me in the eye. 'Basically, Tara, I've had enough of being me.' Her face hardens, her teeth clench. 'I want to be you.'

Some people might take this as a compliment. But coming from Maxie, it sounds like a threat.

She lowers her voice and leans forward. 'So I'm taking *everything* that's yours,' she says through her teeth.

This time there's no mistaking it. That was definitely a threat.

Chapter 21

Family meetings are not as fun as Mob meetings. We're in the drawing room at Mum's house. Not the kitchen, or the TV room, but the posh drawing room. Not a good sign.

For a moment it's like I've travelled back in time three years and everything is normal: Mum and Dad and me and Maxie, hanging out at home. I have to remind myself that Dad doesn't live here any more. I don't think he's been back in the house since the split.

'You're in a lot of trouble, Tara,' says Mum. She's next to Dad but sitting really straight, making sure she's not touching him. Dad has a cup of tea and he's using a coaster, even though he never used to. It's like Dad's a guest here – and not a welcome one – but he and Mum bought this house together. It used to be our home.

'I was trying to help,' I say weakly, even though I know the best way to deal with a telling-off is just to stay quiet.

'But you haven't helped,' Mum says. 'Lying never helps.'

Dad sighs. 'We understand what you were trying to do, sweetie,' he says. 'But you have left us in a very difficult situation: do we tell Mrs Eames at WSG what happened?'

'Of course we do,' says Mum. 'As a lesson in honesty, if nothing else.'

'I think we have to,' says Maxie.

Mum and Dad look at each other.

'OK, we'll tell,' says Dad. 'But that means there is no way they'll take her back now.'

Poor deluded Dad was clinging to that hope. I was at the meeting – it wasn't happening – and that was before this new revelation.

'Maxie seems to have settled in very quickly at Hillcrest,' says Mum. 'She has a lot of friends.'

Her friends, my enemies.

'And it might not be a special school, but it's still a very good school,' she finishes.

'So that's decided then.' Dad throws up his arms.

'What's the matter?' says Mum, frowning at him.

'Forget it,' he says, and stands.

'Where are you going now?' Mum yells after him. She tuts and gets up. 'That bloody man is impossible,' she says. Then quickly adds, 'Sorry.'

She follows him, but at the door she turns back. 'Tara, we'll speak about your punishment later.'

Oh God, what if she grounds me?! The fund-raiser at the nightclub is tomorrow.

'I'll do anything, just don't ground me,' I plead. Reece will be there. Donna will have him all to herself.

'You should have thought of that before you did this,' she says, and she slams the door on the way out.

I did *this* over a year ago. How could I have known then that something I was doing to be nice would come back to bite me?

There's yelling from the kitchen. They've closed the door, but we can still hear them. Maxie and me sneak out, hovering in the hall to eavesdrop on what's happening now.

'. . . doesn't help when you're acting like a child!' Mum shouts.

It's like the bad old days two years ago, just before the break-up. I look at Maxie. We're both so sad. It's funny how I can hate my sister and love her at the same time. We have our messed-up family in common, whatever happens.

'I'm trying, Julie,' Dad says. 'It just seems that as long as you're happy – you three – then it doesn't matter how I feel!'

'It's about what's best for the kids!' she says. 'And after what you did, you don't really have a leg to stand on.'

A pause. Dad's saying something, but it's hard to hear what. But Maxie and I are spying experts – we put our ears to the door, her head just above mine. We've done this loads of times.

'. . . if she doesn't go back to WSG . . .' Dad's voice is shaking. He's gulping as he speaks. '. . . I just miss them both so much. Not living with them kills me.' I start crying, and from the way Maxie's breathing above me, I can tell she's crying too. 'And the fact that it's all my fault makes it so much worse,' he says.

He says it's his fault, but it feels like mine.

Dad's footsteps come towards the door so Maxie and I straighten up quickly. Maxie looks at me. There are tears streaming down her face.

'Max . . .'

But she shakes her head to stop me from speaking. Then she turns and runs upstairs. My heart breaks as I watch her.

Dad comes out of the kitchen. He wipes his eyes with the back of his hand, but it's too late to disguise the fact he's upset.

I can't think of anything to say.

Above us, Maxie's bedroom door slams. We both look upstairs, and Dad gives a quick shake of his head.

'I'm sorry I stormed out again, Tara,' he says.

'I'm sorry I cheated on Maxie's personal statement.'

Between the two of us, Dad and I have ruined this family.

'Don't tell your mother,' he says, putting his arm around me and walking to the front door, 'but I am secretly impressed. They said your personal statement was excellent, didn't they?'

I nod, giving a half-smile.

'It makes me very proud to have two geniuses in the family. Your mother and I are clueless. How you both managed to turn out so great is a complete mystery to me.'

He kisses me on the forehead, then heads to the door. He looks all alone. I call out after him. 'Hey, Dad.'

He turns.

'I think it's best if Maxie and I don't share the same planet tonight, let alone the same postcode. Can I stay at yours?'

He looks back at the closed kitchen door. He's about to say what all parents say when you ask if you can do something. 'You'll have to check with your mother.'

There it is.

I ask Mum, who seems happy to get rid of me after what I've done. Dad buys me McDonald's on the way to his. That he did *not* check with Mum. That one was our little secret.

Chapter 22

Dad drops me at school early the next morning. Everything in my family is just too awful. Being at Dad's is better than at Mum's, and even school is better than home. But things at school aren't great either.

No reply from Abby. Again. This is the eighth time I have called her since last night. I'd hate to think this means what I think it means. The secrets were under lock and key. Donna got them from either Abby or Obi . . . It couldn't be her, it just couldn't be. She's my best friend.

The changing rooms at the pool seem empty, but I think I can hear someone moving around. I follow the noise, passing the sections of lockers – each with benches in the middle for people to leave their clothes on while they dress.

The noise stops. 'Hello?' It's Abby.

I find her in the last section, the one by the door to the pool. She's in her swimsuit. It's new. And only now can I see that she has lost a ton of weight. She looks great, but then she always did. She does look thin though. I'm still worried that it's *too* thin too quick. This is another thing she's been super-secretive about. When we were younger I thought Abby and I would never have secrets.

'Tara,' she says, putting her hand on her heart in relief. 'I thought it was . . . What are you doing here?'

'Why haven't you answered my calls?' I reply.

She picks her phone out of her bag and looks at it. 'Sorry,' she says, 'it was on silent. I didn't realize. What's the drama?'

'Oh, Abby, everything is just terrible!' I wail, hot tears coming instantly. 'All this stuff is going on at home. My parents found out this thing.' She's frowning, but because her face is being pulled back by a tight white swimming hat I can't tell if it's a listening frown or a guilty frown.

'It's all to do with Maxie. Somehow she found my insurance secret – the one that was locked away in the handbook.'

'Oh.'

'Is that it?' I ask, still sobbing. 'Aren't you worried that she might have read your secret too? Aren't you worried that we got the wrong person and Obi is the Mole, not Candy?'

'I was just about to have a swim.' She shoves her clothes in her bag and puts the bag in her locker, so her back is to me.

'A swim?!' I yell. 'What is wrong with you?'

She slams her locker door. 'What is wrong with *you*, Tara?' she says. 'I'm supposed to be your best friend. But here I am, swimming at eight in the morning, and you haven't even asked why.'

'I . . .'

'I have lost ten pounds in four weeks, and you have been too absorbed in your own little world – your club, your petty rivalry with your sister, your dumb crush on Reece – that you haven't even noticed.'

Calling the thing with my sister *petty* is painful. But I know I've been neglecting her. 'I'm sorry, Abby,' I say.

'It's supposed to be mates over boys, but you've put everything over me.'

'I have a lot of stuff going on at the moment.' I need to explain to her. If I could tell her how bad things have become. 'You see—'

'I don't care about your stuff! You care enough about it for the both of us.'

Her *petty rivalry* comment was the starter. That was the main course.

'I have stuff going on too, you know,' she continues. 'My sister is always in hospital. My parents are always with her – they never notice me either. You have a sister who is healthy and a family that is there for you. I have bigger problems than your stupid playground stuff.'

'Oh my god,' I say. 'Is Becky OK?'

'She's fine,' says Abby. 'At the moment. Thanks for asking.' She picks up her towel, spins round and heads out to the pool.

Suddenly something clicks and I work out what's been going on all this time.

'It wasn't Candy, was it?' I say. 'It was you.'

Abby stops in her tracks.

'Were you the Mole all along?' I ask, my voice much more steady than I feel. 'Did you give our secrets to the Club for money?'

Abby nods.

I can't believe it. My best friend sold me out. She let us blame Candy, who was innocent. What's happened to her?

'You sold our secrets just so you could buy some clothes?'

She turns back to me. 'You are unbelievable,' she says, like this is somehow my fault. She pauses and then adds, 'When you next see your sister, please tell her I'd like to join the Club. Not only do they have the quantity, but it seems they have the quality too.'

And there's the dessert. I feel ill. I'm not quite sure what just happened, but I think I have lost my best friend.

Chapter 23

Luckily, when Obi gets my text and meets me in Mob HQ before registration, her reaction is completely opposite to Abby's; she gives me a big fat hug.

'You don't think I've been a bad friend, do you?' I ask her.

'You haven't been a bad friend to *me*,' she says.

'Do you think I have been a bad friend to Abby?'

But I know the answer to that already. I haven't been the *best* best friend a girl could have. I definitely could have done better.

'I reckon best friends need more than other kinds of friends,' Obi says.

She's right, and I certainly haven't been doing that. Abby only joined Hillcrest because I did. We thought it would be great being girls in a boys' school – *scary*, but fun. But the boys were mean. And what did I do? Start a club to make new friends. Like Abby wasn't enough. Perhaps it should have been me and Abby against the world.

Obi puts her arm around me. 'I wouldn't know, because I've never really had a best friend.' She looks me in the eye. 'In fact, that was my secret.'

I'm shocked. 'But, Obi,' I say, 'you're so . . . nice. And fun. And funny.' I think about it for a second. Here I am, suddenly best-friendless. And then there is Obi, who is brilliant, and would really like one.

'Obi . . . If you like . . . we could—'

Obi shakes her head as she laughs at me. 'Don't get me wrong, Tara,' she says. 'It's a nice offer . . . but you and Abby were best friends for so long. I'm not sure I could compete.'

I should feel rejected, but she's right. I could never replace Abby. I just hope I can fix things. 'I reckon I could forgive Abby,' I say. 'If she apologizes.'

'Maybe you should apologize to her.' Obi raises an eyebrow at me.

I'm about to protest about all the horrible things Abby has done, when I stop and really think about it. Yes, she sold me out – literally – selling our secrets so she could buy herself a new wardrobe. But she wouldn't have done that if I hadn't been a terrible friend to begin with.

'I think she'll be back,' Obi says. 'You two have been friends for too long. And until then, we always have the Mob.'

I look down at our new Mob bracelets – three pieces of string plaited together – so rubbish compared to the ones Candy made. Candy, who was innocent all along. Candy, who isn't in the Mob any more. Then I look at the Mob Handbook with the codes in it. The codes Maxie cracked. Maxie who isn't in the Mob any more. Then I see the star logo drawn on to the side of the file. Drawn by Abby. Who isn't in the Mob any more.

'Not much of a Mob now, is it?' I say.

'Don't say that . . .' But Obi trails off, finally counting who's here – just the two of us. 'Come on,' she says. 'Let's see if we can get a drink from the dining room.'

We walk out of the girls' loos and round the corner towards the long corridor where most of the classrooms are. At the end is the noticeboard where the teachers said people are allowed to advertise charity events. I spot our nightclub-night posters all fanned out on the board, and my hopes rise.

'Maybe it will all turn around tonight,' I say. 'Abby will come and we can make up. I mean – who wouldn't want to go to a nightclub?' I imagine everyone dancing, drinking cocktails with umbrellas in the top.

'Did you invite the Club?' asks Obi. The way her voice rises sounds hopeful – she wants them to be there.

'I haven't *not* invited the Club,' I tell her. This is not the same as actually inviting them. 'If everyone goes, maybe they will. Maybe we could all be friends when this is over.'

'Argggh,' she shouts. 'Who would have thought a charity drive could be so cut-throat? I thought it was supposed to be a way for the new girls and the boys to bond, but instead it's . . .'

She's stopped by the sound of running footsteps. Reece comes round the corner and skids to a halt. He stands there looking at us, panting. His hair is even more wild than usual.

Even with everything that's going on, I can't help but smile.

'Hi,' I say. 'What's up?'

'Is . . . everything . . . OK?' he says, breathing heavily. 'I . . . heard . . . yelling.'

Obi and I burst out laughing, the tension suddenly gone. How does Reece always do that?

'What?' he says, and a flop of hair falls over his eyes.

I laugh again. 'Nothing,' I say. 'At least, it's not you.'

'We're fine thanks, Reece,' says Obi. 'What are you doing here? Patrolling the corridors like a knight in shining armour?'

I wish I could talk to boys the way Obi can. I guess it's one of the perks of having brothers.

'Detention,' he says, rolling his eyes. 'For being late. Again.' He checks his watch. 'In fact, I am late for the detention.'

I laugh.

'Hey,' he says, his tone now changed to sympathetic. 'Sorry to hear about your fundraiser thing.'

'What?' says Obi.

'What did you hear?' I ask. Obi and I glance at each other.

Reece tilts his head to one side. 'That tonight is off.' He's figuring out that we're clueless and his jaw clenches. 'I assumed you were the one who cancelled it.'

I can feel myself getting panicky. My fingers start to tingle.

'Who told you it was cancelled?' Obi and I ask at the same time.

He looks back and forth between us. He's not sure what's going on but he clearly guesses it's more serious than a fundraiser evening. 'Umm . . . I dunno. I heard it from Sean Flynn.' Reece scratches his head and his hair gets messier. 'He said he heard it from Maxie.'

And there it is. *I'm taking everything that's yours*.

'You sure?' I squeak. I can only just get the words out.

He nods.

'Who else thinks it's cancelled?' says Obi, looking at me in action-plan mode. 'We have to find out who she's told. Then start damage limitation.'

'Um . . .' says Reece. 'Everyone.' He points down the corridor to the noticeboard.

I run. Obi is right beside me. Before we even get there, we see what they have done, in black and white.

Across our five fanned-out posters, they have pasted one big sign. It reads:

CANCELLED

Chapter 24

We're still standing in the corridor, still mesmerized by the new sign.

'It wasn't like this yesterday. Was it?' says Obi.

I know who did this. She pretty much told me she would.

Obi puts her arm around me. It's only now that I realize I'm crying. Reece comes round my other side and puts his arm around me too. If I wasn't so upset I would be happy that the boy I like has his arm around me.

'Don't worry,' Reece says. 'We can just tell everyone it's back on.'

'We'll put it up on our Facebook page,' says Obi, smiling like Facebook is a magic wand you can wave over everything.

But Maxie won't have made it that easy. 'I bet she'll have called the nightclub and cancelled it.'

'*She?*' Reece asks.

'My sister,' I tell him.

They both look shocked.

'Everyone will think I'm a liar. No one believed I could get a nightclub, and now they'll think I made up the whole thing. Oh God!' It just gets worse. 'We had to put down a £200 deposit for tonight. If Maxie's cancelled the nightclub, she'll have taken that money.'

Obi's eyes go wide. 'She wouldn't steal £200, would she?'

It would be more normal than stealing 1p. But I don't say that.

'You don't *know* Maxie's cancelled it.' Reece is so sweet he's clearly having trouble believing my sister could be this nasty. 'At least call the club and check.'

When Reece says 'the club', I think he means the Club. It takes me a second to realize that I have to call the nightclub. There's a tiny chance this could be fixed.

I look up the Boulevard on my phone, get the number, tap it and it rings.

The nightclub manager was nice when I spoke to her before, but that was when I was asking for a booking, not messing them around.

'Hello, Broadway Boulevard.' The woman's voice is croaky, as if she's been up all night, and given that it's 8 a.m. and she's working at a nightclub, I'm guessing she probably has.

'Hello, this is Tara Simmons.' I put on a voice, trying to sound professional and grown-up, like I've seen them do on *Young Apprentice*.

Reece gives me a thumbs-up, as if congratulating me on my name.

The woman says nothing.

'I don't know if it was you I spoke to before,' I say, 'but I called about the underage party.'

Still the woman says nothing.

'A private hire,' I continue. 'For tonight.'

'What did you say your name was, luv?' she asks.

'Tara Simmons. Or it might be under "the Mob".'

'You want me to check a booking for the Mob?' she asks.

I laugh. I can't help it. I always do when I'm nervous.

'Ha! No. Never mind. It will be Tara Simmons.' I'm waiting for her to tell me nothing's booked for tonight, that someone – my evil sister – cancelled it. 'Or just "Simmons".'

'Oh yeah!' she says finally. 'Simmons. I got it.'

'You've got it? Brilliant!' I give Obi and Reece a thumbs-up back. Looks like we can save this after all! Have the nightclub night, raise loads of money, beat the Club, go to Alton Towers, Becky can get her wheelchair, and Abby and I can be friends again.

'Great,' I say to the woman. 'A few of us will be there at about four o'clock to—'

'Hold your horses,' the woman says. 'I have your name here as a potential booking, but it was never confirmed. We've gone ahead with something else.'

My thumbs-up drops to a thumbs-down. 'We didn't mean to cancel it,' I tell the woman. 'We don't want to cancel it. We're really—'

'What I'm telling you, luv,' the woman says, sounding a little annoyed, 'is that it wasn't cancelled; it was never booked.'

This doesn't make any sense at all. I shake my head at Obi, who is frowning, confused. But I'm just as confused as she is.

'Well, can I get my £200 back then?' My head is spinning with how much I have to sort out.

The woman's voice hardens. 'Are you having a laugh?'

'What? No,' I say. My hands are shaking.

'This is a joke, right?' she says. 'You call saying you're from the Mob, and now you're demanding £200. Nice try, luv. It's *you* who's supposed to give *us* £200!'

'What? But I can't . . .' I've heard nightclub owners can be nasty. 'I'm only twelve.' I let my fake voice go.

'I remember you now,' the woman says, lightening up a bit. 'It was me you spoke to,' she goes on. 'You were very sweet when you called. Said your mum was going to come round with the deposit.'

'Yes. That's me.' I say. 'Only it was my dad who dropped it off.'

'Well, whoever, but I would have told them the deposit was non-refundable when they came . . .'

My heart sinks. The money is gone.

'But they never came.'

'What?'

'I had pencilled you in, but we never got the deposit. That's why we went ahead with another event. It was lucky for us someone else wanted it.'

I don't know how to feel. She must be lying. If she's not lying, it means the £200 isn't gone, and Maxie hasn't taken it. But if she *is* lying, and we did make the booking but she's is pretending we didn't, then she's nicked £200 from me – well, my mum – and I'll look like a liar in front of everyone at school.

I'm not sure what to do. 'Er . . . I'll call you back.' I hang up.

'This is weird,' I tell them. 'It's lucky the Club sabotaged tonight. The woman says they never got the deposit.'

Obi frowns.

'I'm calling my dad.'

He answers on the third ring. 'Morning, Tara, is everything OK?'

'Dad, it's about the nightclub.'

Dad takes a deep suck-in of breath, like he's just stepped on a nail. 'Arggh, Tara. I forgot to tell you,' he says. 'Oh, I feel awful. I went to the nightclub with the deposit, but they were already booked.'

'But they said they would hold it for me!'

'You know what nightclubs are like,' he says.

'Not really, Dad. I'm twelve.'

'Someone else must have got their deposit in before you. Sorry, darling. This is totally my fault. I should have told you. Has your party been ruined?'

'Daaaad!' I whine. This is typical of him! I am about to get furious . . . but then I realize he's actually saved me. The party has been ruined. But not by him. Everyone thinks it's cancelled anyway. No one is coming.

'Sorry, Tata, I—'

'You know what . . . it's fine.' My dad's hopelessness has finally paid off. Life sucks, but Dad has performed damage limitation. 'I was going to have to cancel it anyway.'

'Oh, really?' He sounds glad to be off the hook. 'Why?'

'Maxie . . .' I can't tell him how evil his own daughter is. It would break his heart. First she's a thief – and a weird, messed-up thief who steals insignificant amounts of money just to get caught – now she's a vindictive cow. 'The nightclub was a bad idea,' I say.

'So all's well that ends well,' he says.

'I guess so.' But if ending well feels like this, I can't imagine what ending *badly* feels like.

I tell Dad I'll see him later and turn back to Obi and Reece. 'The competition is over. Our only chance of beating the Club was the nightclub night. They've won.'

'Don't give up, Tara,' says Obi. 'We've got loads of money so far. The Club have raised less than £10 in the last few days. They've stalled at £293.' I love how positive Obi is. 'I know we can beat them. We just need one more brilliant idea.'

'Perhaps you could bet the whole thing on a coin toss,' Reece suggests. 'Double or nothing. Do or die. Go hard or go home.' He's clearly joking.

'I'm not going home.' I try to follow their upbeat example. 'The money is in my locker. Let's count it.'

'Ladies, I gotta leave,' Reece says. He blushes when he says 'ladies' and it makes me like him even more. 'If I'm any later for this detention I will get another detention, and then I will end up in an eternal detention loop.'

'OK, see you around,' I say.

'Let me know what happens.'

Reece races off and we head the other way. We go up to the third floor, where my locker is. It's halfway along the corridor. 'We should have almost £300 by now,' says Obi.

'I reckon maybe more,' I say. 'Abby and I spent Monday night rattling tins in the shopping centre. We definitely got at least another fifty.' I remember how things were with me and Abby just a few days ago – *icky*, but we were still friends. I miss her, even though it's been less than an hour since our friendship ended.

I go to my locker, open it and pull out my bag.

I tap the side pocket where I keep the money.

I can't feel it.

It's not there.

I pull open the zip and check again. *Definitely* not there!

'Don't panic,' says Obi, who can clearly tell I'm panicking. 'You'll have put it somewhere safe.'

I pull out my bag and start searching it, throwing out my books and pencil case and gym trainers. It's now empty, and there is still no sign of the packet of money.

I toss the bag aside and start trawling through my locker.

Obi picks up my bag and looks inside it again.

'It's gone,' I say. I am certain of it now. Everything has left me – the Mob, my best friend, my sister, the nightclub night – why wouldn't the money be gone too?

Obi chucks the bag. 'What the hell!?'

'It was Maxie. All this,' I say, 'is Maxie's fault.' She's the one who got Abby to betray me. She's the one who's been plotting against me – getting her Club to war against mine. She said she'd take everything from me, and now she has.

'Your sister wouldn't do that, would she?'

It's time to tell Obi what I should have told her ages ago. Some stupid loyalty – or maybe it was shame – held me back. 'I never told you why my sister came to Hillcrest High, did I?'

'No . . .' says Obi, eyes wide, waiting for the dark truth.

'Maxie was . . . expelled from her old school.'

Obi's mouth falls open.

I'm not sure if I should say more, but the money is just as much Obi's as it is mine. 'For stealing.'

I didn't think Obi's mouth could drop further, but it does.

'She's a thief,' I tell her, the words pouring out now, 'and she hates me. She might have guessed the combination to my locker, but she wouldn't need to – she could have taken the money from my bag any time.'

I lean my back against the wall and slump to the floor.

'No money, no nightclub, no nothing,' says Obi.

'Oh, we have a whole load of nothing,' I point out.

'And they have everything.'

I nod, and Obi slumps down next to me.

'Tara, don't take this the wrong way,' she says, and I have a feeling there is going to be no right way to take it, 'but the Mob is over.'

I nod. Of course it is.

Since the day she started Hillcrest, Maxie has been waging a vendetta against me. Maybe it started before that – at my birthday sleepover, when she crashed my Mob. Or maybe even before *that*, when she stole 1p to get herself expelled and moved to Mum's house. She said she was jealous of me and threatened to take everything that's mine.

Well, Maxie has come through with her threat: everything's gone. I have nothing now. And she reigns supreme.

Chapter 25

'Daddy!' I shout.

He gets up from the little table in his small living room where he is sitting with his laptop, and closes the lid quickly. He looks worried – probably because I'm bunking off school.

'What's the matter, darling?' he says, hugging me tightly.

There's no safer place for a girl than on her dad's chest. I feel good here and I don't want to stop crying to actually explain what's up.

He pushes me back gently. 'Did something happen at school?'

I nod. 'Someone stole my charity money.' I haven't the heart to tell him who.

'What?' he says. 'That's awful! Are you sure?'

I nod again. 'It was in my bag. My bag was in my locker. And when I went to check it wasn't there.'

Dad sits back down on his chair with a thump. 'Could it have fallen out?'

I shake my head.

'Could someone have picked your pocket?'

'It was in an inside pocket. Zipped up.'

Dad looks across the table, to the blank white wall behind it.

'I was being really careful. It was over £300.'

Dad's head snaps round in shock at the amount of money that's missing.

We both go quiet. Dad gets up and walks to his kitchenette. He puts the kettle on. He has his back to me as the water boils and he pours it into two mugs.

'Have you told the school?' he says. 'Someone might have handed it in.'

I shake my head. 'There's no point.' Maxie will have covered her tracks this time.

'We'll have to call the police.' He doesn't look keen. Maybe he's thinking what I'm thinking – that it was his thieving daughter Maxie who took it. 'Oh, and I'm sorry I forgot to tell you about the nightclub not allowing children,' he says, sitting down hard, his shoulders sagging.

'I thought you said they had another booking.'

'Yes – well, it was both actually. They looked into their licence and they aren't allowed children on the premises, even if they don't serve alcohol.'

I roll my eyes. My dad is so flaky. I know he loves me, but I can't rely on him for anything. But I am too defeated to be angry with him. It's not his fault his daughter is a thief.

'What am I going to do, Dad?' Now it's my turn to slump. 'I raised all this money for Abby's sister, and it's gone. All my friends hate me, and everyone at school will hate me because I promised them a party that's not happening.'

Dad rubs my back as if I'm about to be sick. The way I'm feeling, I just might be. Joining a boys' school was supposed to be brilliant, but it's been nothing but horrible.

'Do you think Rimewood would let me go back?'

Dad laughs gently into his tea and makes it splash up. 'That ship has sailed, I'm afraid, Tara.'

I give a sideways smile back at him. 'Thought you might say that.'

We both go quiet again, thinking. Everything went weird when Maxie started acting weird. If she went back to her old self – the girl who wore the gigantic black jumper with the holes – we'd all be sorted. But something tells me Maxie's old self is in the same place as that jumper – the bin.

'You could still have a party,' says Dad.

'Really?' I say. 'Do you know a nightclub that's available tonight?'

'Well, perhaps not a nightclub,' he says, 'and perhaps not tonight – but you can have a fundraiser anywhere. You can have it here!' He points to the breakfast bar. 'We can have a make-your-own-cocktail bar,' he says. 'We've got just enough space for a dance floor . . . especially if we move the TV into another room.'

Could we do this? This is like the nightclub idea divided by fifty. Would people want to come?

'And if the TV is in my bedroom, we could make it a cinema – show some scary movies or something.'

I am starting to see it. 'I could even do hair and make-up in mine and Maxie's bedroom!'

'Good idea. And I'll dress in a suit, act all tough, and be your bouncer.'

I laugh at the idea my dad could ever be tough.

'Though . . .' I look around at the poky hallway. I think about how it took me an overground train and a bus to get here.

'Maybe it would be better to have it at Mum's . . . I mean . . .' Dad looks hurt whenever we call his old home *Mum's*; it used to be *ours*.

Dad swallows. 'Hmm. Yes, I suppose it might. Let's check with her.'

He picks up the phone and hands it to me.

'Will you call her?' I ask. 'She'll be angry that I ran out of school.'

'Ha! Your mum certainly can be a tyrant when she wants to be,' he says.

He dials the number and I wince, waiting to see if it will be a nice Mum-Dad interaction or a nasty one. He explains to Mum about the stolen money, and the nightclub cancelling on us – which is not exactly what happened, but it gets more sympathy from Mum and she agrees to have a party at her house.

'Yesssss!' I punch the air.

Dad *hmmms* at Mum seriously, but smiles at me and punches the air too. 'I'll come and act as bouncer.'

I can hear enough of what Mum is saying to hear her laugh at that too. But then her tone changes and she's asking a question.

'When?' Dad repeats her question, looking at me for an answer.

Good point. When? 'It needs to be before the end of the month,' I whisper to him. 'So, next weekend.'

'Next weekend?' he says to Mum.

Mum starts speaking really quickly. Again I can't hear the words, only that she sounds agitated. Everything was going so well.

'Sorry, darling, I didn't think,' Dad says into the phone, forgetting that he's not supposed to call Mum darling any more. 'Isn't there something we could do? Could we not include both of them?'

Both of them? What is he talking about? I glare at Dad and raise my arms in a what's-going-on? gesture. He holds up his hand to shush me.

'Aren't they both raising money?' he asks Mum.

Both who? Me and Maxie? She can't be included in this! I shake my head melodramatically so Dad gets the message. 'Not Maxie, no,' I stage whisper.

'That's great then,' he says. 'I'll tell her.'

I cross my arms in front of my chest. They'd better not have done what I think they've just done.

'And . . . I'll . . . er . . . s-s-s-see you next Saturday then,' he says, like he's preparing for a first date.

He hangs up, looking at the phone.

'I'm not sharing my fundraising party with Maxie's Club,' I tell him.

'Tara, don't be selfish.' He gives me a look I haven't seen since I was six and opened all the doors on Maxie's Advent calendar.

'But it's a competition!' I remind him. 'There's no way I can win if they get half the takings from the party.'

'Tara—'

'Someone stole my money,' I say. 'I'm way behind!'

He frowns at me. 'Tara—' He raises his voice, but I can't believe he's being so unfair so I cut him off again.

'Dad! Maxie is trying so hard to beat me that she's stooped to devious levels. She stole my ideas, she stole my friends. She's a selfish—'

'Tara!' Dad is properly yelling now. 'You've forgotten something.'

'What?'

'Next weekend is Maxine's birthday.'

Oh.

Maxie is exactly eleven months older than me. There are only thirty days between our birthdays. Next weekend is 30 September.

'Can't we have two parties?' I ask him, my voice quiet. 'One for the fundraiser on Saturday and one for Maxie on a different day?' But that sounds ridiculous, even to me.

Dad shakes his head. 'You can have your party,' he says, 'but you'll have to share it with Maxie and her friends.'

The war is really over now. The Club have beaten me so badly I'm not sure I'll get over the trauma.

And now I have to help them arrange the victory parade.

Chapter 26

It's five days until the party and I'm supposed to be handing out invitations during break. But there's no point. Instead I head for the girls' toilets to hide.

When I open the door I hit something.

'Ow!'

Some*one*.

'Sorry,' I say. *Please* don't be someone from the Club.

And it's not. It's the quiet girl – Simone. The girl who hasn't joined any clubs since she started here. I don't think I've seen her say one word to anyone. She's friendless. Just like me.

'Didn't mean to smack into you. Are you OK?' I ask her.

Surprise, surprise, she doesn't say anything, so I just walk by her and head for a cubicle.

'Are *you* OK?' she asks. Her voice is really quiet. Probably because she never uses it.

'I'm fine,' I say, turning back to the toilet.

'That's what you want everyone to think, isn't it?' she mutters.

'What?'

'Nothing.'

She's right. If I could just swallow my pride and tell my sister how I feel, beg her to stop this . . . or even tell Mum Maxie stole from me. But this situation reminds me of the time I got stuck in a toilet cubicle at a restaurant: there were loads of people around, but I was too embarrassed to call out. I struggled and struggled, pulling at the lock, but it wouldn't open. Eventually I waited for everyone to leave and slid under the door – getting muck all over my top. Probably not the most mature way to deal with things.

Instead of telling this to a stranger, I say, 'Do you want to come to my fundraising party?' and thrust an invitation into her hand. 'It's only £5 to get in.'

God, does that sound like the most desperate sentence a girl has ever said? Thing is, I have twenty-five invitations to hand out and no one to hand them to.

'What is it?' says Simone, not even looking at the invite.

I'm guessing it would take a lot of convincing to make a girl like Simone come out of hibernation, and my piece of paper won't be enough to convince her. I don't have Abby's design skills. I just typed the details of the party and printed them out on coloured A4 paper. Hardly very exciting.

'We're turning my house into a major fun zone.' (Does that sound fun, or really rubbish?) 'It costs £5 to get in and then £1 to enter each room of the house, and there will be something going on everywhere: we've got a cinema . . .' (My sister's room with the TV set up in it.) 'An arcade with a casino . . .' (The dining room, where we'll have a pinball machine, a computer game, and Maxie's going to run a roulette wheel.) 'A beauty salon . . .' (Me, my hair tongs and my make-up bag in my bedroom.) 'A cocktail bar . . .' (My mum in the kitchen making fruit drinks with umbrellas in.) 'And we've hired a famous DJ for the nightclub room.' (Just the living room, but there will be a real DJ there.)

'Didn't you lie about hiring a nightclub last week?'

Turns out Simone doesn't speak, but apparently she does listen. 'No . . . I . . . I didn't lie.'

'Thanks, but no thanks,' she says, giving back the invitation.

'But loads of people are coming!' I say enthusiastically. This however *is* a lie. At least, I have no idea how many people are coming. The worst thing about having the party at home, rather than a nightclub, is that Mum will only let us invite fifty people. Each person has to have a proper invitation or they can't come into the house.

So I'm allowed twenty-five invitations and Maxie's allowed twenty-five invitations, and we're splitting the proceeds. But because I have no friends, I haven't handed out a single flyer yet. I wish I'd just cancelled the whole thing.

'Please come.' Now I have resorted to actual begging. 'All the money goes to charity.' I shove the invite at her again and the word *charity* means she has to take it or else she's a bad person.

'It's on Saturday,' says Simone.

'Is that a problem? Are you busy?' Suddenly I am really intrigued about Simone.

'No, I just meant . . . Isn't that the same night as your sister's party?'

I don't believe this. 'It's the same party! Her birthday and my fundraiser combined.'

Just then the door opens and Simone has to jump out of the way. It's the people I most don't want to see – the Club – with my sister at the head.

'Hello, Tara,' says Hannah. 'Talking to yourself now?'

'No, actually.' I point to Simone who's standing behind the door.

The other girls look at each other. Everyone else is as intrigued about her as I am.

'Oh, hi, Simone,' says Sonia.

Maxie steps towards her. 'Is Tara telling you about my birthday party?'

'I was just giving her one of my invitations,' I say, smiling. I can't show that I've been beaten. 'For the *fundraising* party.'

Maxie ignores me.

Simone frowns. She's not intimidated by us – right now she looks like the most confident person in the room. 'Aren't you twins?' she says to Maxie. 'If it's your birthday, isn't it Tara's too?'

Brilliant! Simone has just gone from stranger to *perfect* stranger. She's caught Maxie out in her lie. If

I'm Maxie's twin, like she's been telling everyone, it's as much my party as it is hers. No one had the brains to work this out earlier. Not me, not even genius Maxie. Now the girls in the Club look confused. Hannah and Candy look at Maxie to explain it for them.

I just stand there with a smug grin on my face. It's a small win, but I'll take it.

'Aw, bless.' Maxie's only wrong-footed for a second. 'Did you hear that silly rumour?' She says this to Simone, but everyone is dying to hear. 'We're not really twins.'

'*Pfft!*' Explain your way out of this one, big sis.

Sonia gasps. Donna hides her surprise. Hannah and Candy look at each other, each checking that the other was fooled too. Only Abby knew the real truth all along. But Abby's got that blank look on her face – the one she's been wearing for weeks.

'We're not twins,' Maxie says again. 'It's just something Tara likes to tell people.'

Excuse me!

Surely they must remember back to the beginning of term. It was *Maxie* who told everyone we were twins – she told them she was the evil one.

But the Club are hanging on her every word. 'It's a game me and *Tata* used to play – you know, when we were babies.' Maxie does a stage whisper, half covering her mouth, 'But I think we're a bit old for it now. Don't you?'

Donna and Sonia snigger.

I am fuming. All this time she's told everyone she's my twin. Now she's taking it back, she somehow makes *me* look stupid.

'I'm the older sister,' she adds. The Club nod at each other as if that's obvious. 'Older by eleven months.'

'Seems like more, doesn't it?' says Donna.

Just when I think my sister can't stoop any lower, I find out evil has a basement level.

'Simone will want one of the proper invitations,' says Indiana. Her bag is decorated with peace symbols – pretty ironic – and she takes out a glossy flyer with a photo of Maxie on it, her face superimposed on a roulette wheel on one side and a DJ's turntable on the other. It's just as cool as the one we made for the nightclub night.

'Did you make this, Abby?' I ask her.

'Yes.'

Ten years of best friendship and now all I get is one word.

'But the invitation I have will get you in too,' I say.

Donna sneers at my crappy A4 invites.

It feels as if Simone – who has kept herself out of everything – is going to be the one to judge us. But when we turn back to her . . . she's gone.

'Oh.'

From the looks on everyone's faces, none of us saw her leave. We were so wrapped up in ourselves she managed to slip out of the door without us noticing.

I'm getting out of here too. 'You might as well have these.' I dump my invitations into Maxie's hands. 'Go ahead and invite who you like. You'll steal anyone I bring anyway.'

Hope that hit her where it hurts – letting her know I know she stole my money like she's stolen all my friends.

'You not with Obi?' Maxie asks. If I didn't know better, I would think she sounded concerned.

'No,' I say. 'She's not in the Mob any more.'

'Interesting,' says Donna. 'A new recruit for the Club.' She knows how much this will wind me up.

I wish I could do now what I did that day in the restaurant cubicle. Sneak under the door and slip out after everyone's gone. It might not be mature, it might make me dirty, but it sure would be easier. Simone is actually really cool – by leaving like that she made our war seem petty. Why does it seem like such a big deal to me? Why do I want to win so badly?

Thing is, I don't even know what winning would look like any more. Either way, as I walk by myself into the corridor, I definitely feel like a loser.

Chapter 27

There is a steady *whump whump whump* coming from downstairs in the nightclub room – aka the living room.

I'm all alone in Tara's Salon – aka my bedroom. I have all my hair and make-up stuff set out on my dressing table – even some magazines by the bed as a waiting area. But not one person has come upstairs since the party started. There are fifty people coming tonight and forty-two of them are boys. Boys don't do hair and make-up. How did I not think of that? This is a lame idea which will raise zero money.

Worse still, I am miles away from Reece. I've played straight into Donna's hands. She's probably somewhere snogging him right now.

That does it. I scribble a quick 'Back in 5 minutes' notice, Blu-tack it on to the door and head downstairs.

Dad's manning the front door, wearing his best suit. He has plastic tubs in front of him set up to take people's entrance money.

He waves at me. 'You having fun, sweetie?' he says.

'Yeah! Great!' No need to bother him with the truth.

I walk into the nightclub room. We spent the morning moving all the furniture to one side so there is loads of space to dance. We've turned off the main light and set up some disco lights at the side that send coloured dots flying across the walls. Even though the DJ hasn't arrived yet, people are dancing to the playlist Maxie made. Judging by the way everyone is jumping around in there, it's going down really well.

I see Reece. Thankfully he's not snogging Donna Woods. Not yet anyway. He's moshing with Joel and Lenny.

'Hi, Reece,' I say.

'Hi, Tara! Awesome party!' He shouts as if he's in a nightclub, even though the music's not that loud.

'Thanks!' I say, getting into it and shouting back. 'I didn't know you liked this kind of music. Thought you were more indie.'

'Normally, yeah,' he says, bobbing his head in a distinctly un-dance-move kind of way. 'But your sister has such cool taste.'

'Oh. Thanks.' *I think.*

'Where are the girls?' Lenny says, sticking his head between me and Reece.

The Club haven't arrived yet – I know this because the noise levels aren't high enough. There are only boys here.

I ignore Lenny's question and shake a tin in Reece's face. 'Would you like to make an extra donation towards my charity?' We're splitting the proceeds for tonight. Mum and Dad have spoken to the school about the missing money, but unless it turns up the only way I can beat the Club is by getting £300 in this one little tin. I have more chance of finding a £300 note on the pavement.

'Sorry.' Reece shrugs and turns it into a shrugging dance move. 'I already lost all my money at the casino. We were betting with sweets, and what I didn't lose to the house, I lost to my stomach. Your sister is a like a wizard as a croupier.'

My sister. Again. Everyone thinks this is my sister's party. And from the *Happy Birthday, Maxie* banners everywhere, I can't really blame them. I told Mum the banners would take the focus away from the fundraising – but she said it was Maxie's birthday and one or two reminders couldn't hurt.

Well . . . It hurts. I don't know why I'm even here.

'Better go and check this casino out,' I say, trying not to show how depressed I am. 'See if I can win some of your sweets back.'

I walk from the nightclub room, looking for someone to talk to. I wonder if Simone decided to come. She had an invitation, but I can't see her. It's like she doesn't care about having friends. I wish I felt the same way.

In the casino room Maxie's standing there in one of my pink prom dresses. It's something she would never have worn a few months ago. She's running the roulette table, throwing in the ball and spinning the wheel. It has a hypnotic effect on everyone. Including Dad.

'Dad,' I say.

Maxie gives me a filthy look, as if she thinks I shouldn't be here.

I ignore her. 'Aren't you supposed to be bouncing?' I say to Dad.

'Er . . . yeah . . . I just . . .' He doesn't take his eye off the wheel. 'After this round.'

'Aren't you supposed to be hairdressing?' Maxie says to me.

The doorbell rings. Dad doesn't react. 'I'll get that, shall I?' I say.

Dad flaps at me. *Great. Thanks, Dad.*

I really hope this is the DJ arriving. He said he'd play from 7 p.m. until 10, which is when his shift at the nightclub usually starts. He's already half an hour late.

I go to the hallway, but Kyle Rosen has got there before me and opened the door, throwing it wide and letting in whoever is there, totally ignoring Mum's sign telling people not to do exactly that.

'You can't let them in unless they have an invitation!' I yell.

But now the door's open I see it's Obi. We've hardly spoken all week and I'm so pleased to see her. I rush forward. 'Obi!'

Obi's wearing tight jeans and a sparkly top. Her hair is loose and straightened and I've never seen it like that before. She's even put on a bit of make-up and painted her nails.

She adds her five-pound note to the tub, smiles briefly and then her smile drops – as if she's correcting a mistake.

'How are you?' I ask her.

'I'm good,' she says, looking behind her. 'Yeah. You?'

'I'm OK,' I say. 'The party's OK . . .'

Obi is still looking behind her.

'Did you come by yourself?' I ask. 'You didn't bring Bem and Jumoke?'

'They're coming,' she says. 'But separately. I don't want anyone to see me with them.'

'Ha!' I say. Good old Obi. She never changes. Maybe I'll be able to salvage at least one friendship out of all this. 'Come on in,' I say. 'My mum's running an invent-your-own cocktail bar in the kitchen. Only a pound.'

'Erm . . .'

'There's also a casino in the study that Maxie's looking after. Dad's supposed to be the bouncer but he's bounced off. And I'm running a beauty salon upstairs – although you look gorgeous.'

'Er . . .' She's squirming. 'I'm sort of waiting . . .'

'For who?'

But she doesn't need to answer. Outside, the noise level goes from bird screech to security alert at the British Museum. Six girls emerge round the gates of the house, arm in arm and singing one of the tracks that has been playing and replaying on Maxie's iPod all night.

The Club. I've never seen them so dressed up. I'm guessing they've been at Candy's house getting ready, and Candy's older sister has been helping with their hair and make-up. Which totally makes my hair salon a waste of space. They look like a girl band – not quite matchy-matchy – but each of them has one item of pink, so you can tell they're a group. Sonia has pink highlights in her hair. Even hippie Indiana is wearing a long necklace of pink beads around her neck. They look great – but I'm more jealous of the fact that they look like friends.

Abby's there, and something presses on my heart. She looks amazing. She's got a pink skirt on and a black strappy top. Her arms are covered in body glitter and she looks fab. I've always thought

Abby was beautiful – but that was because she was my best friend and I loved her. Now that we're not best friends I realize how *actually* beautiful she is.

I look back at Obi and catch sight of her nails. Her newly painted *pink* nails. The exact same shade of pink that the rest of them are wearing. There's even nail art on one of them. It's a Club symbol.

'Obi . . .' I don't believe this. 'Have you joined the Club?'

'Um . . .' She looks at the floor. 'Sorry, Tara. But I really, *really* need friends.'

I need friends too. Who doesn't?

There's a scream from behind me. 'Girlies!' It's Maxie, running to the front door and pushing right past me. Borrowing my pink dress now makes total sense.

There is more screaming and air-kissing as they hug each other. Donna pulls Obi in too, and I can see Obi smile, eyes closed in delight.

'Happy birthday, Maxie!' they yell together.

Now all the boys in the corridor are crowding round too. Somehow an impromptu *Happy Birthday* starts up, with everyone clapping along. Maxie's cheeks go pink – perfectly matching her dress.

She curtsies. 'Thanks, everyone,' she says. 'Welcome to my party.'

I am invisible. I press myself against the wall so the Club can fit in. There is lots of oohing as they take in the decorations and the signs everywhere pointing out what's going on in each room.

'Has the DJ arrived?' asks Donna.

'I want to get a photo with him,' says Sonia.

Maxie checks her watch. 'He should be here by now.'

'DJs are always late,' says Indiana, and all the girls nod along even though I'm pretty sure that none of them has ever encountered a real-life DJ before.

Maxie's looking around and finally notices me. 'Where is the DJ?' she asks.

I shake my head. All of the girls in the Club stare. Donna and Sonia look me up and down. Hannah's ponytail is higher than ever. In my jean shorts and lace-lined V-neck I feel really under-dressed.

'How should I know?' I say, putting my hands on my hips and trying to act like none of this bothers me.

Donna scoffs. 'I bet she never got the DJ,' she says.

There's a buzzing in my ear. Everyone is looking at me and laughing.

'Just like she never got the booking at the Boulevard nightclub,' she continues.

This is so unfair. I thought we had booked the nightclub. We *definitely* have booked a DJ. I spoke to the guy myself. But the way everyone is acting makes me doubt my own mind.

The buzzing in my ear is starting to make me feel dizzy. 'I . . .' People from other rooms have come out to watch my public humiliation.

'You've completely ruined Maxie's birthday party,' Donna adds.

'It's not . . .' I want to remind Donna that it's not just Maxie's party. But Mum always says, *If it looks like a duck and it quacks like a duck, then it's a duck*. This party is certainly quacking like it's Maxie's party.

'Tara tells lies to make herself look good,' Donna announces to everyone.

I can feel myself turning bright red, not the cute pink that Maxie's gone.

'Because her dress sense isn't enough to make her look good.'

It feels like she's murdering me. And no one's doing anything to help.

'Tara is a liar, *and* a loser, *and*—'

'Oh, shut up, Donna.'

Donna flinches like she's been slapped.

By my sister.

'Tara isn't lying,' Maxie says. She looks me in the eye. 'It's not her style.'

I should be happy that Maxie is sticking up for me. I *am* happy. But weirdly, it makes me want to cry.

I can't decide whether to hug Maxie or hit her. I have so much to say – to her and Donna – that I find I can't say anything.

Instead I run.

'I didn't realize Tara had style,' Donna mutters as I leg it up the stairs.

'Tara has more style in her little finger,' says Maxie, 'more style in the *cuticle* of her little finger, than you could have in a lifetime.'

I'm in shock. I've been saved by my worst enemy. The girl who stole from her school, then stole my friends, then stole my charity money. My life has been ruined and it's her fault. Maybe she's got one of those split-personality things. I don't understand how she could betray me so badly and then stand up for me like this. It doesn't make sense.

I keep on running, ignoring the people lining the stairs who are trying to speak to me. My plan is to wait out the night buried in my loft room until it's over. But as I pass Mum's room I see the light on. Someone's in there, even though there's a 'Keep Out' sign.

I open the door. 'You're not allow—'

It's Dad, on the laptop.

'Oh. Sorr—'

Dad's always on his laptop. I guess he has to check his emails all the time in case someone's looking for a photographer.

But then I spot what's on his screen: a simulation of a roulette wheel. It's spinning.

Dad closes the laptop.

'Why are you playing up here?' I ask him.

'Erm . . .' He's clenching his teeth.

'You can play for real downstairs,' I remind him. 'And, even better, for sweets.'

'Of course,' he says. 'Give me a sec and I'll come down.'

He's trying to get me out of the room, and quickly. I don't get it.

Then suddenly it all starts to make sense. Everything that's happened. All the money that's gone missing. All the stuff that's gone wrong over the past few weeks – maybe even the past few years.

The divorce. Maxie's attitude transplant. Everything.

It's not Maxie's fault.

It's Dad's fault.

My dad is the person who stole the charity money. He did it to fund his gambling addiction.

Chapter 28

Dad slams his laptop shut quickly. 'What are you doing in here? Why aren't you out there enjoying your party?'

'What are *you* doing in here?' I ask. My voice is low, steady. This is not a question, it's an accusation.

'I'm . . . checking emails,' he says, standing up hurriedly. I did not see emails on his computer screen. 'You'd better go back down. People will be wondering where you got to. The hostess . . .'

'Dad . . .' I start, but there's a big angry lump stopping the words getting out. I take a deep breath. There is no way to say it except just to say it. 'Have you got a gambling problem?'

As much as I'd like to, I can't take the question back.

'No,' he says, opening his arms out wide, slightly shocked. '*No!*' he gives a half-laugh. 'Why would you say that?'

For a moment I actually believe him. Wishful thinking.

'Let me see your computer,' I say, taking a few steps closer, reaching for the laptop.

He shields it from me. 'No!' Then he changes tack. 'Just because I like to place a bet once in a while, doesn't mean I'm a gambler.' But he fumbles over *gambler* like it's too big for his mouth.

I change tack too. 'The DJ isn't here,' I say to him.

'Er . . . um . . . You know what DJs are like.'

This is what he said about the nightclub.

'Not really, Dad,' I chant, monotone. 'I'm twelve.'

He laughs. But it's forced. He tries to get by me.

'Have you got his money?' I ask, blocking him by putting my hand out.

'I . . . er . . . I already gave it to him,' he says. 'If he doesn't show then I'll get it back.'

I hate catching Dad out in his lie. Part of me wants to pretend everything's OK. But that would be sliding under a cubicle door rather than asking for help. You might get away, but not cleanly. 'I spoke to the guy myself,' I say. 'He said we could pay cash when he got here.'

Dad looks at the space past me. 'I think . . . I don't think . . .' But he hasn't worked out how to complete this sentence.

'And as you didn't manage to book the nightclub last week,' I say, 'can I have the £200 back?'

'I gave it to your mother,' he says.

'I can ask her for it, can I?'

The door opens and we both spin round. Maxie comes in, looking concerned. 'Are you OK, Tara? Don't worry, I gave Donna hell. I told her . . .' She picks up the mood in the room. 'What's going on?' she asks.

Dad claps his hands together. 'Now I remember! I *forgot* to give the deposit back to your mother. It's at my flat. I can go and get it if she needs it.' He tries to leave. 'I'll get it now.'

He's not going to admit it. Not unless he has to. Instead he's going to run away.

'What's going on?' Maxie asks again.

'Maxie, I need you to tell me the truth about something.' I give her a look that I hope says, *For once, sister, act like my sister*. 'Did you take my charity money?'

'No!' Her eyes are wide. 'I didn't even know it was missing . . . Has someone stolen your money?' She is looking me in the eye, not blinking as she says it.

'Yes,' I tell her.

She covers her mouth with her hands. 'All those hundreds of pounds?' she asks.

I nod and I can feel my lip wobbling. 'I assumed it was you. Because, you know . . . But I believe you if you say it wasn't.'

She looks at me sideways. 'That's very nice of you,' she says. 'I don't think I would believe me if I were you. Not with my track record.'

'I believe you because . . .' I close my eyes as I say the words, 'I think it was Dad.'

I wait for Maxie to shout at me, to have a go at me for being the most horrible disloyal daughter a man could have.

'Was it you, Dad?' she says quietly.

'No . . .' he says. Then louder. 'It really wasn't.'

Maxie grabs his arm. 'Dad,' she says, 'want to know how I worked out how to steal money from WSG's bank account?'

Dad hangs his head. I have no idea how she did it. But it seems Dad knows exactly how.

'I learned from you,' she says.

What? Dad taught Maxie how to steal from an internet bank account. Why?

'I did it the same way you stole from Mum.'

Chapter 29

'You stole from Mum?!' I yell at my dad.

Whens and hows and whys are flying round my brain. There is no way that Dad stole from Mum. But then I remember that he stole from me, from the charity. And that's the lowest of the low.

Dad exhales heavily.

Maxie grabs his laptop from under his arm and he doesn't even try to stop her.

'Let me show you.' She starts up the computer and logs on to a bank's home page. She then types in some numbers into the personal banking login.

'What are you . . . ?' Dad starts, outraged. 'How do you know my PIN?'

'Because you are not as cunning as you think you are,' she says, without taking her eyes off the screen.

While the bank's website looks complicated to me, she navigates around it like an expert. She types in the date of the statement she wants to see. Two years ago. A month before Mum and Dad told us they were breaking up.

'Look.'

£1,000 goes into Dad's account, from Mum's account.

'That was a maintenance payment,' Dad says. 'You know she gives me money every month.'

'Look at the date.'

It was before they divorced. A month before.

'She flicks back another month. A similar transfer, £1,600 this time. The month before, £700. Before that, £900.

'Stop.' I don't want to see any more.

'Your mother approved all of those payments,' he says. 'I just . . .'

He turns to the closed door. I hear it too: heavy steps. We all look at each other, panicked. It can only be Mum.

'Tara? Maxine?' she calls.

This is the moment. The moment where it all comes out.

‘Where are you?’ she says. ‘I heard an argument downstairs . . .’ The door opens and she puts her head round. ‘What are you three doing in here?’ she says.

Maxie finally says what’s needed to be said for a month now. ‘Mum, I never told you why I stole 1p from the school bank account.’

Mum takes hold of the door frame to steady herself. Part of me wants Maxie to stay silent. This is too big.

‘I transferred 1p from their bank account into mine because I *wanted* to be caught. I am not the only thief in this family . . . But you know this.’

Mum closes the door quickly and leans her back against it.

‘It’s why you and Dad split up,’ she continues. ‘Because you found out Dad was stealing from you.’

They never told us why they were breaking up. They didn’t say because Mum didn’t want us to think badly of Dad.

‘Look what you’ve done, Bill,’ she whispers.

Dad covers his ears like he’s caught in an explosion. ‘I’m sorry,’ he says. He starts to cry. ‘I need help.’

I hate him for what he's done. But I also want to save him. 'He does have a reason,' I tell them. 'But it's not a good one.'

Mum and Maxie look at me expectantly.

'Dad has a gambling problem,' I say.

I motion to the laptop. Maxie passes it to me. I get to the browsing history and a list of the past ten websites pop up.

WilliamHill.com

888.com

Casino.com

Maxie and Mum can see it all. Mum sighs. She clearly had no idea. But it's all making sense now. Why he stole. Why he sometimes has loads of money, sometimes none. Why he always shuts down his computer whenever we walk into the room.

Maxie flops forward. 'I'm supposed to be a genius, so how did I never . . . ?'

Mum puts her arm around her. 'This is not your fault!' she says. 'I was married to him. How did *I* not know?'

I look at Dad. He starts pacing.

'Bill? Is it true?'

Dad stops. Looks up. Looks down again. Maxie grabs my hand.

Finally, he says, 'Julie, I ruined our marriage by stealing from you. I lied to you too.' He lets out a big sigh. His voice breaks as he says, 'I lost my family. It's the worst thing that's ever happened to me. And it's all my fault.'

Mum tries to touch him on the shoulder, but Dad changes direction and paces away.

'I am a gambling addict.'

He sits heavily on the bed. Mum waits a second. She closes her eyes as if hearing it again in her mind. When she opens her eyes, there are tears. I'm crying too.

My dad is addicted to gambling. This is something I have heard on TV and stuff, but I never knew what it looked like. I wonder what could be so exciting about gambling – so much that my dad could steal from his wife and lose his children – and yet still carry on doing it. I'm furious.

But right now, he looks like a child. He's not enjoying this. He didn't want this.

'I'm really sorry,' he says, and he lifts his head enough so that I can see him. 'I messed up as a husband. I've been a terrible father. To you especially, Maxie. When you were living with me I told myself I could control it. But I failed.'

He begins to weep, his shoulders shaking. This is too much. How can we ever get over this? What's going to happen to him?

'I even made you lie for me,' he says to Maxie.

Maxie bites her lip.

'You're better off living with your mother,' he finishes.

Maxie walks over to Dad and hugs him. Dad starts to sob in her arms. This isn't how it should be; Dad should be looking after *us*, not the other way around.

Mum comes over and hugs me. 'It's OK. We're going to help your dad get better.'

The music downstairs is still thumping. Mum looks at the door. 'Girls, will you be all right if your father and I go for a walk?' she asks.

We both nod. 'We can man the cocktail bar,' I say.

'Together,' says Maxie.

I'm going to close the casino room. It doesn't feel right now.

Mum smiles. 'You're good girls.'

She helps Dad up. Dad wipes his eyes on his sleeve and Mum waits with her hand on the door for him to be ready.

'Dad,' says Maxie as he's about to leave the room, 'did you take Tara's charity money?'

Dad turns and looks at her. 'I didn't. I promise.' He looks at me now. 'I had no idea you had that much. If I did, I might have taken it.'

That's an answer so scary it must be true.

We watch them walk across the landing and down the stairs. Mum is leading Dad like he's an invalid. I feel as if I have grown up five years in the last five minutes. I don't think Mum and Dad are going to get back together any more – I'm not that naive. But maybe if Dad is truthful with Mum now, they can at least get along.

Even after all he's done, I feel sorry for him. He's so alone.

Maxie is still deep in thought. 'If Dad didn't take your money, and I didn't take your money,' she says, 'who *did* take it?'

Suddenly it's obvious. The girl who has been acting so weird recently. The girl who's changed –

her looks as well as her personality. She sold our Mob secrets to Donna. She knows my locker combination. She was at school the morning the money went missing.

My former best friend.

'It was Abby.'

Chapter 30

Abby betrayed the Mob, betrayed me and stole the charity money we raised for her sister.

'But why?' asks Maxie.

I would think she was able to read my mind if it wasn't such an obvious question.

'I don't know,' I say. 'I need to speak to her.'

There's a huge crash from below. It sounds as if a table full of drinks has fallen over.

'Uh-oh.' We leg it from the room. At least Mum insisted we used plastic cups.

We're only halfway down the stairs when we hear another crash.

'I'm seeing a pattern,' says Maxie. 'Don't say it's apophenia.'

'Er . . . Who?' Maxie's genius means she sometimes comes out with these weirdo words.

'It means seeing random connections when . . . oh, never mind.'

In the hall everyone has gathered around the door to the nightclub room, looking in. Some people are smiling kind of wickedly, but what's more concerning is the people looking worried.

'Tara! Maxie!' Reece shouts from further down the hall. He's running. 'I've been looking for you everywhere.'

'What's happening?' I ask, as we jump the last two steps down to him.

'You better get your mum and dad,' he says.

Maxie and I exchange a panicked look. 'They're not here,' she says.

'They've gone out . . . somewhere . . . for a minute.'

Reece doesn't bat an eyelid at my non-explanation. The music changes to some sort of metally grunge that Maxie used to like – it's dark and screamy.

'Phone them – now,' he says.

'Why?'

'Craig Hurst is here.'

Oh God.

There are more raised voices coming from the casino room.

'And he's brought his friends.'

This is bad. This is exactly what Mum didn't want.

'How did they get in without invitations?' says Maxie.

'They had invitations,' Reece says. 'All of them did.'

'How . . . ?' I say, clenching my teeth. But it doesn't really matter how. They're here and we have to get them out.

I look into the nightclub room. When I left it, the dance floor was filled with people. Now it's just Matt Higgins and Mo Hussain. Mo has taken the disco lights from the floor and put them under his T-shirt so the coloured dots are making patterns through the material.

Donna and Sonia are at the side of the room. Donna with her hands on her hips and Sonia copying her, only looking more afraid.

'Put the music back,' says Donna.

'Yeah,' says Sonia. 'Maxie made a playlist.'

But Mo is too busy concentrating on his T-shirt. He tucks the base of the light into the top of his trousers, then moves his arms around like a robot.

I burst into the room. Maxie is right behind me. 'Change the music back!' I say.

'Er, no,' says Matt. He stands in front of the iPod dock so I can't get to it. 'We're enjoying this.'

'Stop being selfish!' I go to reach around one side of him, but he steps across to block me.

Maxie approaches. 'You're ruining the party,' she says. She tries to reach around the other side of him. He stumbles back a little and bumps against the sideboard. The iPod shifts and he turns around quickly to stop it falling off, like he's suddenly remembered how to behave. But as he flips round he knocks over a cup. A full one. It sprays all over the iPod and the dock and the speakers and the plug sockets.

There's a spark and the music stops. The lights go out. People start screaming and laughing.

'What have you done?' I yell at him.

'Er . . . sorry . . .' he says.

But then Mo comes over, laughing. 'Mate, you totally killed the music!' Which makes Matt laugh too.

'Get out. Now,' I say, using my scariest voice.

'OK,' says Matt.

I can't believe it's that easy.

'Just let me get a drink first,' he adds.

It's *not* that easy.

Obi runs in behind me. 'Tara,' she says, 'it gets worse. Come!'

She leads the way. Loads of people are in the hall and loving the fact that the electricity has gone. We can just about see, and a few people are using their phones for light. Someone has opened the front door and people have spilled out on to the driveway. It's eight o'clock and soon we'll be in complete darkness.

In the casino room Phil Horner is standing on top of the roulette table. His shoes are making scuff marks on the expensive green velvet. Everyone's sweets from the betting are on the table and he's stepping on them – grinding them in.

Obi rushes ahead of me. 'Get off!' she shouts. 'Before I push you off!' She swipes at him but only manages to bat his shin.

I lurch forward and grab her by the shoulder.

'Don't,' I say. 'He's not worth getting hurt for.'

'I'm not so sure about that,' she mutters.

Phil grins at me. 'I'm going to try my luck!' he says. He bends down and takes a handful of sweets from the dealer's pile and puts them all on number 21. 'My lucky number,' he says. Then he spins the ball around the wheel.

There are still some people in the room. They don't know whether to watch or run.

'Get down, loser,' I say. 'You weren't invited.'

'Loser?' he says. He picks the ball up from the roulette table and places it on number 21. 'The house always wins!' He laughs. 'What are the chances?'

'Thirty-seven to one,' says Maxie. 'Idiot.'

Phil frowns. He wasn't expecting an actual answer.

'Boys like this feed on attention,' I whisper to Maxie and Obi, 'like zombies feed on brains. We don't have to get him out, just get everyone else out.'

While Phil jumps off the roulette table to see what else he can destroy, I signal to everyone else in the room. There are only a few people left – Hannah, Candy and a few of the boys from our year. I twitch my head to the door and they all leave.

'Awesome!' he shouts. 'Pinball.' He starts whacking at the buttons on the side. Then picks up the machine and holds it on a slant so the ball doesn't fall down the hole.

Meanwhile the room has emptied.

'Bye, Phil,' I say.

Phil twists round. He drops the pinball machine, gutted that there's no one watching him perform.

I start to close the door. 'You stay here,' I say.

'Wait!' he shouts, and dives towards me. But he's too far away. I shut the door and Obi, Maxie and me hold on to the handle as he tries to pull the door open.

The handle rattles and moves, but he's no match for the three of us.

'Fine!' he shouts. 'I'll just eat all these sweets, shall I?'

'Help yourself,' says Obi.

We all grin at each other. One down, three to go. Speaking of three . . . 'Where's Craig?' I ask.

If his cronies are acting this badly, I can't imagine what Craig is doing.

'I'm calling Mum,' says Maxie, getting out her phone.

We didn't want to disturb them, but I reckon they'd prefer to cut their walk short than come home to annihilation. 'Good idea,' I say. 'I'm going to look for Craig. Obi, stay here and make sure Phil can't get out.'

'Got it!' she says, saluting me.

The fact that I can't see or hear Craig makes me more nervous than if he was right in front of me spraying graffiti on the wall. I decide to look in the absolute worst place he could be: the posh drawing room.

I walk towards the front of the house and my fears are confirmed. The lock at the top is unbolted. I guess my parents never figured *some* babies come in taller packages.

The door is ajar.

I push it open. The room's a mess. He's thrown the cushions on to the floor and now he's lounging on one of the sofas – dirty shoes resting on the arm.

'What are *you* doing here?' I ask him.

He grins at me. He's so glad I've caught him. 'That's no way to speak to a guest,' he says.

'You're not a guest,' I say. 'No one invited you.'

He sits up, putting his feet on the antique coffee table, and reaches into his pocket. 'That's what you think.' He pulls out a piece of paper. A glossy, printed piece of paper with Maxie's face superimposed on a roulette wheel.

There is no way Maxie would have wasted an invitation on him.

'Who did you nick that from?' I ask.

'Careful of throwing around accusations,' he says, putting his hands over his heart. 'Someone gave this to me.'

'Who?'

He smiles. 'Abby.'

Chapter 31

Does Abby fancy Craig Hurst? That would explain a few things she's done recently . . . always being spotted with him, losing all that weight, the personality change.

'Is Abby your girlfriend?' I ask him.

'Flabby Abby?' he says. 'Don't make me sick.'

Which blows that theory out of the swimming pool.

'Whatever,' I say to him. 'I don't care who invited you. This is my house, and you have been *un*invited.'

He stands up. 'Shame that the nightclub thing didn't happen last week,' he says. 'I heard it was cancelled.'

'Someone told everyone it was cancelled . . . but it wasn't . . .' Then I realize the truth. Maxie said it wasn't the Club who put the 'CANCELLED' sign up, and I didn't believe her. But it wasn't the Club who told everyone.

'It was you!' I yell. 'You're such a pig.'

'Aw, don't be angry. You have a pretty cool party here,' he says, and takes a few steps towards the mantelpiece.

In my head the mantelpiece has an invisible perimeter around it to stop anyone going near Mum's collection of Venetian glass figurines.

'You have a dance room, a casino room, a cinema . . . but you are missing one thing.'

'Get. Out.'

'A circus room,' he says. He puts his hands on the mantelpiece and my stomach churns.

'Don't touch that stuff,' I say. 'They're my mum's. They're really old and expensive and—'

'Bet you didn't know I could juggle, did you?'

My heart rises in my chest. He picks up one of the ornaments: a miniature glass bottle. He throws it up and catches it.

'My parents will kill you,' I growl at him.

'But they're not here, right?'

He throws the bottle up really high. I dive forward. *Please let me catch it!* I can hear my heartbeat in my ears. My hand closes and I feel the glass in my palm. Relief washes over me.

'Guess I'm not as good a juggler as I thought.' He throws another one – this time a little rocking horse. 'Guess I need to practise.'

I have to lurch left to catch it. I just manage to, but as soon as I do, he's picked up another one. A penguin – my favourite. He throws it high.

There's nothing I can do. I have a glass ornament in each hand already so I don't have an empty hand to save it. I put the rocking horse in my left hand, but it's too late. The penguin is going to smash.

But then a bright streak of blue dashes past me. It's Reece! He catches the ornament.

'Reece!' I say. 'Nice one!'

'Get out, Craig. No one wants you here,' Reece says in a scarier voice than I have ever heard him use.

'Who's going to make me?' he says.

Reece hands me the ornament he has just caught, then squares up to Craig. 'Me.'

Craig looks from me to Reece. He's trying not to look scared, but he's sweating a little. He looks behind me and I see the door to the drawing room is open; people are looking in.

'Whatever.' He pushes past us, and Reece lets him go. 'This party is lame. I'm leaving.' He walks out the door and slams it behind him.

Finally I can exhale. 'Thank you,' I say. 'That was amazing.'

'Couldn't leave you to deal with him all by yourself now, could I?'

I want to relax, but I'm here alone with Reece and that's always made my heart rate rise. We put the ornaments back on the mantelpiece in a neat row.

I look at the rest of the room. 'Mum and Dad are going to kill me,' I say, picking up the cushions from the floor.

Reece looks at the footprint on the arm of the white sofa. 'I'll make sure you get a decent funeral,' he says.

This makes me smile, despite everything.

The door opens and Mum rushes into the room. 'Tara!' She doesn't look angry, she looks worried. She pulls me into a hug. 'Are you OK? Your sister said you had gatecrashers.'

Out in the hallway I can see Dad escorting Mo and Matt out of the house, and people grinning as they look on.

'We've got one in here too, Mr Simmons!' shouts a voice that can only be Obi's.

'Sorry, Mum,' I say, looking around at how messy the posh drawing room is.

'It's fine, darling. I'm just glad you're OK.'

Maxie walks in with Obi, Lenny, Joel, Hannah and Donna. 'You all right, Tara?' Maxie asks.

I nod. 'But the party is ruined,' I say. 'We might as well tell everyone to leave.'

'You don't have to, sweetie,' says Mum.

Dad walks in behind her. 'It doesn't have to be over.'

I look at Maxie. 'It's your party, Max. What do you think?'

She looks around and sighs. 'No DJ. No electricity. The place has been wrecked. Let's just tell people to go.'

'Nooooo,' everyone says at the same time.

'But we don't have any music,' I say. 'Those morons killed the iPod.'

'Er . . . perhaps we could help,' says Reece, going to stand beside Donna. 'Our instruments are at my house round the corner. We could set them up in the garden. You have a few solar-powered lights out there. All we need is electricity for Donna's mic, and we're ready.'

Could this work?

'I'm sure the neighbours wouldn't mind us running an extension cable from their house,' says Dad. 'As long as the music doesn't go on too late.' Dad has already made for the door. 'Are the extension leads where they always were, Julie?' he asks Mum.

Mum looks at Maxie. 'Is this what you'd like?'

Maxie looks at me. 'Only if Tara does. It's her party too.'

Everyone waits for my answer: Reece, Donna, Lenny, Hannah, Mum and Maxie.

I smile. 'What are we waiting for?'

Chapter 32

We've all relaxed a little now. The fifty people still at the party are the people who are supposed to be here. Everyone's helping to set up the outside lights. Mum has worked her magic and got all the guests into the garden with fruit cocktails in their hands. Sucker Punch are setting up their stuff at the back of the garden, Dad's dragged a lead over from next door and Donna is doing a sound check. Even singing the words '*testing, testing*' she sounds amazing.

Maxie hands me the end of a string of fairy lights that we normally use for Christmas, and we start weaving them into the bushes and plants on one side of the garden.

'Ready?' I ask Maxie.

She nods.

I plug the fairy lights into one of the sockets of the extension lead and they glow. The garden looks really pretty. And with Sucker Punch warming up on the patio it's beginning to look like an outdoor festival.

Donna steps away from the mic and nods at the band. They nod back and Donna calls, 'I think we're OK to start playing.'

Maxie stands beside me. 'Shall we tell her?' she says.

'Hang on a second, Donna,' I say. 'Girls.' I look around for the others – Obi, Sonia, Indiana, Candy and Hannah are right here. They've been working harder than anyone. They come over to the stage, right by Donna.

I motion to Maxie, allowing her to break the news.

'Ladies,' she says, 'the war between the Club and the Mob is over.'

'But seeing as it's just me in the Mob, I'm guessing you already knew that.' I laugh, but the others are not sure yet. Candy gives a nervous giggle.

'We are the only girls in a school full of boys,' says Maxie, 'and we should stick together.'

'Yeah,' I say. 'I mean, some boys are OK.' I can't help but look over to Reece, who is busy practising a drum rhythm. 'But some of them are horrible. No need to name names.'

'And absolutely all of them are just plain weird,' says Obi.

'Hey!' says Lenny.

'Get back to work,' says Obi.

'So instead,' Maxie says, 'we've started a new club.'

'And we want you all to join,' I add.

All of them instantly start smiling. And from the way their shoulders sag, I know they're smiles of relief.

'Even me?' asks Donna, cringing a little.

'Yes. Even you,' I say.

With everything that's going on with my mum and dad, Donna's the least of my problems.

'Thanks,' she says. 'And I'm sorry about earlier. I was a cow. I was jealous.'

Why would Donna – with that hair – be jealous of *me*?

'Do you forgive me?' she pleads.

'I'll work on it,' I say. It's the best I can do.

'Thank God,' says Obi.

'So if we're a new club, what are we called?' asks Candy.

That's a good question. I look around at the girls, trying to see if they have any inspiration. It's only now I realize that Abby's not here. Where is she? I haven't seen her since she arrived.

'I've got it,' says Indiana. 'The Boys' School Girls.'

'Does exactly what it says on the tin,' says Obi.

'We sound like a girl group,' says Hannah.

'That's a good thing!' says Candy.

'The Boys' School Girls – awesome,' says Maxie. She opens her arms wide and everyone jumps in for a hug.

Everyone except me. 'Where's Abby?' I say. 'She should be here too.'

The others look around.

'I haven't seen her in ages,' says Indiana.

'Maybe she went home,' suggests Hannah.

'Between us girls,' I say, 'I'm worried about her. She betrayed me – and she wouldn't do that for nothing.'

'Sometimes people do bad things as a cry for help,' says Maxie. She's talking about Abby, but I get the feeling she's talking about herself as well.

'Does anyone know what's up with her?' I ask.

Blank looks.

'Erm, I have an idea,' says Donna. She looks as if she's in pain. 'I feel terrible, because I paid her to do it, but we *do* have a copy of her secret. Maybe if we found out what it was, we would know how to help her.'

'Donna, that is a genius idea.' I know it's bad to read people's secrets, but something's up with Abby and she might need our help.

Donna gets her bag from the side of the stage and hands it to Maxie. 'My phone's in here. Use your whizz-kid powers to save our friend.'

Maxie nods.

'I'll help, Max,' I tell them. 'You guys start playing.'

'I'll help you too,' Obi says to me.

Maxie, Obi and I head over to the corner of the garden. We pull out Donna's phone and a pad of paper. There is just enough light to see by. We flick through the photos on Donna's phone to find the one of the secret piece of paper.

There's Abby's secret, below mine and Obi's:

KZIQO PCZAB QA JCTTGQVO UM. PM QA JTIKSUIQTQVO UM NWZ UWVMG.

'How do you do it?' I ask Maxie.

'Yeah,' says Obi. 'How do we work out which letter is *A*?'

I'm glad to see Obi's as clueless as I am. And I'm a little excited. It's not often I get to see my sister's genius in action.

'Good evening, everyone! How are you doing tonight?' It's Donna, calling out to the crowd like we're at Glastonbury and not in my back garden.

Maxie ignores the concert going on around her and has started scribbling on a piece of paper from Donna's notebook. The girl is like a machine. 'We don't need to start with *A*. Once we figure out one of the letters – *any* one – we have them all.'

'OK, but how?' I ask.

'It starts with a little guessing.'

One of the partygoers knocks into me as people close in to listen to Sucker Punch.

'Sorry for the delay in setting up tonight,' Donna continues. 'We're almost ready to go.'

I have to block out the party and concentrate.

Maxie points at one of the words. 'When you see a two-letter word like this, it's likely to be a one of few words: *an, is, at, to* . . . that sort of thing. If it's *an*, then the coded letters should be fourteen letters apart. Does that make sense?'

'Um . . .' says Obi, frowning so much her eyebrows nearly cover her eyes.

'We're Sucker Punch, and tonight is our very first gig,' Donna continues, and the crowd whoops.

'I think I follow,' I say.

'But the first thing we look for is *ing*. Check the last three letters of every word. If the word ends in *ing*, the second of the three letters should be five places after the first. And the third should be two places in front.'

I stare down at the code, but my brain is taking its time to kick in.

'Yes!' says Maxie.

'What?'

'Look,' she says. 'The two longest words –' she points them out: JCTTGQVO and JTIK-SUIQTQVO – 'they both end in *QVO*. They could both be *ing* words.'

I count it on my fingers. '*V* is five letters after *Q*.'

‘And *O* is two places back,’ says Obi.

Maxie smiles. ‘We’ve done it.’

Wow, she makes it seem so easy.

‘But before we start,’ Donna shouts into her mic, ‘our drummer has an announcement to make.’

I look over. The drummer never goes front of stage. What could he want to say?

‘Now we have *I* and *N* and *G*,’ says Maxie, ‘it’ll take no time to work out the rest.’

‘No time?’ I ask, my eyes still on the stage as Reece gets up from behind his drums and walks over to Donna’s mic.

‘No time,’ says Maxie. ‘See – I have already got the rest of the alphabet.’ Her piece of paper is covered in letters.

‘OK, so that first letter is . . .’ I run my finger over the new alphabet she’s written out. ‘*C*. Then . . .’

‘*R*,’ says Maxie. ‘*A* . . . *I* . . .’

‘Tara Simmons, where are you?’

I gasp. Reece is calling me to the stage. Maxie and Obi look up from the piece of paper. They have a look that reminds me of how my parents used to look when I was about to open a present.

'What do I do?' I whisper.

'Go on,' Maxie whispers back. 'We can take care of this.'

Obi takes me by the shoulders as if trying to shake some sense into me. 'If you don't go to him now, he'll never ask you again.'

I feel all fluttery inside. Clearly Maxie and Obi think Reece is about to do what I dare not hope he's about to do.

'Good luck, sis,' Maxie says, and squeezes my arm.

I stand up and take a deep breath. I walk forward slowly through the crowd around the stage. Everyone's looking at me, as intrigued as I am. Maybe he's not going to do it. Maybe he's just going to thank me for throwing the party. Maybe I'm delusional to even think he's going to ask me out.

'Tara?' Reece calls again, pushing his floppy hair out of his eyes and squinting into the crowd. 'I hope you're here, or else this is going to be embarrassing.'

This gets a little laugh from the crowd.

Candy and Indiana have found me and they drag me to the front.

I put up my hand. 'Um . . . hello,' I say, but my voice won't come out normally.

Indiana nudges me. 'Louder,' she says.

'I'm here!' I shout.

'She's here!' shouts Candy, grabbing my arm and waving it around so Reece can't miss me.

He crushes his lips on one side. He looks nervous, he looks excited, and he's looking right into my eyes.

'You're a hard girl to track down,' he says. 'But now you can't move.' He looks back at Donna, who nods at him. 'Donna and I have written a duet.'

Donna? Maybe this has nothing to do with me.

'And it's dedicated to you,' he says.

Did he just say . . . ?

Indiana turns to me, her eyes massive. 'That's so romantic!'

Joel and Lenny start playing their guitars – a sweet, melodic tune, nothing like the stuff I heard them play before. There are no drums as Reece is craning over the mic that Donna is holding for him.

'Unbelievable,' says Hannah.

'Donna told me they've been practising this for days,' says Sonia.

'She has,' says Candy. 'I've overheard her singing through the walls.'

Wow. This is huge. Reece likes me as much as I like him. I feel so lucky. Donna and Reece start to sing:

> '♫ *I'd kinda like to be more smart*
> *To know how to protect*
> *My fragile heart.* ♫'

Aww, how cute is this? He can't have written it for me.

> '♫ *But if I had only one wish*
> *It's that you would be my first kiss.* ♫'

He looks right at me when he says this. I don't believe it.

'Not to ruin the surprise,' Candy says, 'but he's going to ask you out after the song.'

Right now I love Candy for her nosiness.

'Tara!'

There is movement behind us. Maxie and Obi are pushing their way through.

'You have to come, quick,' Obi says.

'She's being serenaded!' says Indiana.

I glance up at the stage and Reece is facing Joel and Lenny as they give a little guitar riff.

'We've decoded Abby's secret,' says Maxie. She's gone a bit pale.

'It's bad,' says Obi.

'What is it?'

Maxie shoves the piece of paper into my hand. I can just make it out in the light. It says:

> Craig Hurst is bullying me. He is blackmailing me for money.

Oh God. This is awful! But it makes total sense now: why she's been acting so different, losing weight and stealing. This must be why people keep seeing them together.

'We have to find her,' I say.
The second verse starts up.

'♫ *I can't do magic, but if I could*
I'd transport myself to where you stood. ♫'

Reece looks down at me again. His smile drops when he sees my expression has changed. He fumbles his next line.

'♫ *I'd like to . . . um . . . chant . . .* ♫'

But like a true professional he carries on.

'♫ *Like you enchant me.* ♫'

I turn around and see Sean Flynn standing behind me. 'Sean, have you seen Abby?'
Sean smiles and wiggles his eyebrows. 'When everyone came out here she went up into one of the bedrooms . . . with Craig Hurst.'
Oh no.
'But Craig was chucked out,' says Obi.
'Nah, he hid from your dad in a wardrobe.'

That sounds like Craig – coward.

I shove everyone aside to get back into the house.

'Tara, you can't go now,' says Hannah. 'Reece is singing you a song.'

'He's going to ask you out,' adds Candy.

'You're going to publicly humiliate him!' says Indiana.

I turn back to look at Reece. He's frowning at me, but trying to sing.

'♫ *But if I had only one wish*
It's that you would be my first kiss. ♫'

My heart squeezes to the size of a pea.

'I have to help Abby,' I say as I turn away from the stage. 'It's mates over boys, remember?'

This time I haven't forgotten.

Chapter 33

I hope it's not too late. I hope, whatever he's doing, he hasn't hurt her.

'We should split up,' says Maxie.

I didn't even realize she was behind me. And the rest of the Boys' School Girls have followed too. We rush from the garden into the house.

I stop for a moment by the front door. 'Good idea,' I say. 'Obi, you keep trying Abby's phone. Has anyone got Craig's number?'

Hannah nods and looks disgusted with herself. 'We did a project together in English. He made me do all the work, of course.'

'You call Craig and see if you can find out where the scumbag is.' I think of the layout of my house. 'Indiana and Sonia, you search this floor. Maxie, search the second floor. I'll go to my room.'

This feels like a moment for a handshake, but there's no time.

I run up the stairs all the way to my loft room. It's just my bedroom and a small toilet room up here. I'm sort of hoping I find them, but also hoping Abby's left and she's safely home with her family. But as soon as I get there I can hear her crying.

'But I've done everything you asked,' she whimpers.

'And now I'm asking for more,' he growls.

I am so angry I could kick the door down.

'Get away from her!' I yell.

They both turn. Craig has his back to me while he towers over Abby, who has pressed herself into a corner of the room.

Craig sneers. 'Make me.'

I walk towards him, scowling. I'm a little out of breath, but nothing's going to stop me. 'What do you want from her?'

'Fat tax,' he says, laughing.

I have never heard anything so disgusting. I want to punch his lights out.

He waves his phone at me. 'I'm protecting the world from this hideous sight.' It's a photo on his phone, but I'm too far away to see what it is. 'Makes me sick every time I look at it.'

Walking forward, I can now see it's a photo of Abby. She's in the changing rooms at the school pool. She's only got her bra and skirt on. And you can tell she has no idea someone is taking a photo.

'You pervert!' I yell at him.

Abby cries harder. This must have been that day she texted me about someone hiding in the changing rooms. The day I ditched her to hang out with Reece. I never asked her about it. I'm so angry – with myself as much as with Craig.

'I'm telling Mr McAdam,' I say. 'And Mrs Martin. And they'll probably tell the police.'

'You wouldn't dare,' he says. He's turned away from Abby now and is heading for me.

'Why wouldn't I?'

'Because one tap of this button and the picture's on Facebook. A couple more taps and I can email it to everyone at school.'

'You're a pig,' I say to him.

'Don't speak to Abby like that.' He laughs.

Abby cries again. 'Please don't wind him up, Tara. I would die if anyone saw that photo.'

I don't want to give in to blackmail, but the expression on Abby's face says nothing would be worse than people seeing her picture. 'How do we get you to delete it?' I ask.

'At first he said I had to give him £20,' says Abby. 'I thought I would easily be able to pay it back. I wouldn't have taken money from Becky's fund for nothing. So I gave him £20 . . . and he wanted more.'

'This photo is worth hundreds,' said Craig.

'Even when the price went up to £300 – and I gave it to him – he *still* wouldn't delete it.'

'You made her give you the money meant for her own sick sister?'

'Talk about sick?' he says, waving the phone. 'This is sick.'

'Once he had *all* the money he said I had to print him invitations to this party, and that would be the last thing. So I did.' Abby hangs her head. 'Now he still wants more.'

'Another £100 and it's yours,' Craig says to me. 'A rich cow like you should be able to get that, no trouble.'

I don't know what to do. We've probably raised £100 from tonight, maybe more. But I know what will happen; if we give him that, he won't stop.

‘No way,’ I say. ‘Hand over the phone or I’m calling the police.’

‘Leave the room and I hit “Share”.’

I want to call Mum and Dad, but they are all the way in the garden. I make a split second decision and I run at him, snatching at the phone. ‘Give it!’

He pushes me, hard. I fly backwards and land on the floor. The impact reverberates through my bones.

‘Loser,’ he says, walking towards me with his fist raised.

This is it. I’m about to get punched. I wince, preparing myself to get hurt.

‘Get away from her!’

It’s Maxie!

She rushes in and slams him back with all her force. He falls on to the bed.

Maxie is followed by Obi, Candy, Hannah, Indiana, Sonia and even Donna.

‘Call your witches off,’ says Craig, sitting up. He’s still holding the phone, his finger just over the Share button. The girls crowd around him. ‘Tell them to back away or I’ll do it.’

'Maxie, we need to delete a photo from his phone. He won't do it unless we give him £100.'

'Yeah, genius,' he says. 'I heard you're some kind of gifted geek or something. Well, work your way out of this one.'

'Just because he's such a thicko,' says Obi.

I throw her a look. This is not the time.

Maxie thinks for a minute. 'Want to know the truth?' she says. 'I'm not really a genius.'

'That's not what I heard,' he says.

'I'm not a genius,' she says, 'but I *am* psychic.'

The girls gasp. 'Is this true?' asks Candy.

'Whatever,' says Craig, narrowing his eyes.

I have to hide my smile. I know exactly what she's up to. Maxie *is* a genius. 'Shhh! You know you're not supposed to say,' I tell her, doing my best to sound worried.

Craig sneers. 'You don't expect me to believe you're a mind-reader, do you?'

The girls look back and forth between Craig and Maxie like it's a tennis match.

'Most people don't,' says Maxie, 'and that's how I get away with it. I'm not that clever, but I pass all my exams and stuff by reading the examiner's mind.'

'You're lying,' he says.

'She's psychic,' says Abby, sniffing back tears. 'I've seen it.'

She *has* seen it.

Everyone goes silent for a minute. They're all trying to work out whether to believe her.

'If I can prove it,' Maxie says, 'you have to delete that picture of Abby from your phone.'

Craig thinks about this for a second. 'And if you can't?'

'We'll give you all the money the Club has raised,' I say, looking at the girls. Who look back at me as if I've gone mad.

'Wait—' says Donna.

'*And* you can post that picture online,' says Abby.

Craig looks unsure but really wants to test this out. Or maybe he just wants the money. Either way, I think he's going to go for it.

'How do you prove it?' he says.

Maxie thinks for a moment, 'I don't know . . .' She scratches her head and quickly winks at me.

I step in. 'How about this: you write down a word on a piece of paper – any word. Then Maxie has to tell you what it is.'

'Wait . . .' says Maxie. 'I'm not sure my skills are that powerful yet. I need—'

'I knew this was a lie,' says Craig, pleased with himself.

'OK,' says Maxie. 'I'll try.'

She closes her eyes and turns her back to us. Craig turns his back on her too, grabs a piece of paper from my dressing table and writes something.

'We need to see it,' I say, 'so you can't say she's got it wrong when she's got it right.'

He gives a smug smile. 'Happy to,' he says, and hands the paper over.

He's written 'Dumb girls', which earns him a growl from Obi, and is also two words, but we don't point that out. Maxie's psychic powers will still work.

'OK,' Craig says to Maxie, 'what did I write?'

Maxie starts pacing back and forth, rubbing her temples. 'Give me a second,' she says. 'I have to get in the zone.'

'Don't forget everything your psychic guru taught you,' I say to her. 'You need to empty your mind.'

Maxie closes her eyes and nods rhythmically.

'Maxie's mind-reading is awesome,' Abby says to the girls. 'Blow you away.'

'Is it really real?' whispers Donna.

'Can you be quiet, please?' Maxie snaps. 'I'm trying to concentrate.' She rubs her temples harder. 'I feel like you are trying to make me feel stupid, an idiot . . . *dumb* . . . Wait.' She opens her eyes. 'Is that in the message?'

Hannah gasps. Craig is doing his best not to look nervous.

'Go on, Maxie,' I say.

Craig's eyes are as wide as two footballs. At this point I am ready to burst out laughing, but I manage to keep a straight face.

'I believe in you,' says Abby.

'Shut up, you two!' Craig says.

'Right you are,' I say.

'Shut your faces now, or I'll cancel the deal.' He looks really threatening.

I give Maxie a wide-eyed look. We've done all we can. Hopefully the trick has worked.

Maxie collapses on to the floor, holding her head. 'Would someone get me a drink of water, please?' she says.

I step forward to grab the glass on my dresser, but Craig stops me. 'I don't want you passing anything.'

Little does he know the *thing* has already been passed.

'Tell me what I said in two seconds, or you owe me that money. And this monstrosity' – he points to Abby – 'is going viral.'

'You . . .' says Maxie in a shaky voice, 'called us . . . *dumb girls*.'

Craig's jaw falls to his chest. 'Wha . . . ?'

The girls gasp again. Hannah covers her mouth with her hand.

'How . . . ?' asks Candy.

Maxie shrugs. 'Gifted, innit.'

'I don't . . .' says Craig.

I take advantage of Craig's stunned state to lunge forward and grab the phone from his hand. I press the bin symbol to delete and OK to confirm. Abby makes a noise that sounds like she's sucking back jelly, but she's sucking back relief.

'And you'd better give back all the money you stole,' I tell him, 'or Maxie will read *your* mind and put *your* disgusting thoughts on the internet.'

'You wouldn't dare!' he says. Then he tries to look tough. 'And anyway, I don't have disgusting thoughts,' he adds quickly.

Maxie pulls a face. 'Yes, you do. Eww, how could you?' she says. She's bluffing, but it works. If this past month has taught me anything, it's that we all have secrets – Craig's are probably worse than anyone's.

'See you first thing Monday morning with all the cash,' I say. 'Now leave my house before my dad catches you up here.'

Craig grabs his phone back from me and runs out of the room.

As soon as we hear his footsteps on the landing downstairs I run to hug Abby.

'Are you OK?'

She nods, but there are tears streaming down her cheeks.

The rest of the girls are hanging back, afraid of Maxie all of a sudden. 'That was amazing,' says Obi.

'Are you really psychic?' asks Donna.

Maxie looks at me and we both laugh. 'Nah, it's a trick Tara and I have been doing for years. Abby was in on it too.'

'Did you hear what we were saying as Maxie was doing her psychic thing? *Don't* forget . . . *You* must . . . *Maxie's* mind-reading . . . *Blow* you away . . . D. U. M. B.!'

They start laughing.

'That's brilliant!' says Donna.

'We are *so* doing that on my brothers,' says Obi.

'Thanks for coming to save me,' Abby says to me.

'What are best friends for?' I reply. But then I feel bad – I should have been there for Abby a lot earlier. Like Obi said, I need to apologize. 'I'm sorry I haven't been a good best friend recently, Abs. I've been so wrapped up in myself that I haven't noticed anything – what was going on with you . . . or Maxie . . . or my dad. I've been an ego-head and I'm sorry.'

Abby hugs me. 'Best friends again, yeah?'

I nod.

'And I'm sorry too, Tara,' says Maxie, joining our hug. 'For everything.'

'Well, thanks for stepping up,' I say to her. Then I can't help but add, 'Eventually.'

'I guess it's the big-sister thing,' she says. 'I get all protective when people are mean to you.'

I want to forgive and forget, but I don't know if I can trust her again. 'But, Max,' I take a deep breath. '*You're* mean to me.'

She hesitates before saying, 'I know. I'm sorry. I guess that's a big-sister thing too.' She pulls at a strand of her hair. 'Today is my birthday. The day I turn thirteen. I'm not your twin any more, I'm your older sister again. It's time I started acting like it.'

I'm not sure if I want to let her off. I'm not sure if I can. But then I remember what Abby said to me in the girls' changing rooms, what Maxie and I have both been forgetting. We've got each other: sisters. Both of us healthy. And we might live in two separate houses – but we're here whenever we need each other.

'Do you forgive me?' she asks.

I'm not sure yet.

'Please,' she begs, and her nervous grungy scowl is back. I thought it died with the gigantic black jumper. I don't want to see either again because Maxie's confidence is good for her. She'd be great if she kept the confidence and returned to the nice person she used to be. I'd love to have my sister back.

'OK,' I say.

Maxie hugs me tighter. Then the rest of the Boys' School Girls pile in too. It seems the war really is over. With us all looking out for each other, we can handle anything.

Bring. It. On.

Epilogue

'The absolute best thing about it,' says Obi, 'is the way Craig Hurst won't come within ten metres of any of us.'

Reece laughs.

'I've actually seen him run out of a room when Maxie comes in,' says Donna.

'It's hilarious,' says Sonia.

We're walking along one of the main paths in Alton Towers. Indiana said she wanted to try the Air roller coaster first – apparently it's supposed to be like flying.

We called the inaugural meeting of the Boys' School Girls first thing on Monday morning. Actually, it was second thing. *First* thing, we got our money back from Craig.

He apologized to Abby and said he knew what he'd done was really mean. He actually blubbed when he begged us not to tell on him. He said his parents would kill him if he got expelled and they didn't have the money to send him anywhere else. We said we'd think about it, and put it to a vote. The deciding vote went to Abby. She said she'd let him off if he gave us £33.74.

That was the amount us girls in Year 8 needed to hit £750. Exactly the amount needed to buy Becky her wheelchair. And also the winning total. I guess this is what happens when you work *with*, rather than against, each other.

And that's the new plan, us girls sticking together. I still haven't managed to convince Simone to hang out with us, but I'm not giving up on her. Not until she sees how great having a strong group of friends can be.

'It's such a shame Abby and Hannah couldn't make it today,' I say, thinking of them too.

Both of them are on family holidays this half-term, but Abby's been texting every hour to see what's going on with me and Reece. I also have her friendship bracelet – with a silver disc that says '*Best Friends*' wound into the strings. We gave each other matching ones. I wear mine with my Boys' School Girls scoobie.

'Yeah, it is a shame . . .' says Donna. 'But then you boys wouldn't have been able to come.'

Donna looks at Lenny and bats her eyelids at him. He grins. Looks like Donna is over Reece and has moved on to her next victim – sorry, *crush*. Sometimes I forget that Donna and I are friends now.

Reece hasn't really spoken to me since I ran away in the middle of his romantic serenade. He blushed a little when I asked him if he'd like to take a place on our winning Alton Towers trip. He said yes, but he hasn't said another word to me.

Not to worry – we have a Mission. I have one wish . . . and the girls are going to help me make it come true.

I summon a little coughing fit. The girls nod.

'Mum, Dad,' says Maxie, shoving the map of the theme park in their faces, 'which is the quickest way to the Air ride?'

Mum and Dad stop walking and look over the map together. It's really great seeing them getting on. Dad's been going to Gamblers Anonymous and he's started counselling too. Mum's been going to some of the sessions with him – not to get back together, Mum's made sure we know *that's* not going to happen – but to help them to move forward. I'm proud of Dad. I'm proud of both of them really.

'This is the quickest way,' says Mum, 'through the gardens.'

'Are you sure?' says Maxie.

Dad looks at the park ahead of us. 'The gardens are down a steep slope – I think it's best to go round.'

Maxie winks at me. Mission accomplished.

'Yes, you're right. Let's go round,' says Mum. She walks on, Donna links arms with Lenny, dragging him along too.

Reecce goes to follow the others, but I pull him back. 'Come on. Let's go through the gardens.'

'Huh?'

'We'll race them.' I push him towards the entrance. The girls have agreed to distract my parents so they don't realize I've gone. This is exactly what the Boys' School Girls are about: looking out for our friends.

It's a warm day, but it's a lot cooler down here in the shade of the trees.

Reece is walking quickly. I guess he's trying to race – like I said – which means there is a slight flaw in our Mission plan.

'Hang on,' I say to him. 'I want to talk to you.'

He waits for me to catch up.

'Did you have fun at my party?'

'It was OK, yeah,' he says. Then he adds some more cheer to his voice. 'It was good . . . you know, apart from Craig Hurst and the others nearly demolishing your house.'

'Thanks for helping me out there,' I say, and I nudge him with my arm.

'No problem.'

He's not going to make this easy on me. And after bailing, I don't really blame him.

'And thanks for getting Sucker Punch to step in and save the night. You were excellent.'

He mumbles something.

'What?'

'How would you know?' he says, sounding put out. 'You didn't hear us play.'

I stop and stand in front of him. 'I heard a little bit,' I say. We're in a shaded spot, I look around and there's no one coming. This is it. 'I heard the part about you wanting to kiss me. Er . . . I mean – the girl in the song.'

Reece can't quite make eye contact. 'You were the girl in the song.'

I move to the side so he has to look at me. 'I *was*? Am I not any more?'

He says nothing.

'If I was the girl in the song . . . this would be a really good place to . . . you know . . . kiss her. If you wanted to.' My ears feel like speakers, streaming out my heartbeat for him to hear. There is a chance he might tell me to shove off. He might want to totally humiliate me, given that I totally humiliated him.

'If I had one wish,' I tell him, 'it's that you would be my first kiss.'

He straightens up. I do too and I look in his eyes.

He nods. 'OK,' he says.

I blow out all my breath. I didn't even realize I was holding it, but I am so nervous.

Reece looks really shy. Which is great because I feel really shy too. He said, '*OK*.' We're actually going to kiss. This is scarier than any roller coaster.

We both lean forward. I close my eyes. Our lips touch and we kiss. Quickly. Then we kiss again, this time more slowly.

I open my eyes for a second, just to see if he has his eyes closed, and he does. I shut my eyes again and relax, trying to let my nerves go, just concentrating on the kissing. It feels amazing.

Finally we stop and I pull him further down the path. 'Come on, before my parents notice we're gone,' I say.

He scurries to keep up. 'Does this mean you're my girlfriend?' he asks.

I beam at him. 'What do you think, silly?'

He kisses me again, this time for longer. I never want it to end. My parents can wait. My friends will cover for me. That's what the Boys' School Girls are for.

Don't forget to look out for the next book in this brilliant series!

SPRING 2015

lilchase.com

quercusbooks.co.uk